"I thought you'd turn me down flat"

Sara stared open-mouthed at her husband. "But Rede, when I did refuse, you persuaded me...." With fingers on her trembling lips she faltered. "You didn't want me to accept. You'd have thought more of me if I'd said no?"

He nodded. "If you'd said 'Go to hell' and meant it, I'd have respected that."

"And you married me, despising me... oh!" Sara turned away, drained of all hope for the future. But he reached for her and took her in his arms.

She looked up at him and cried, "Rede, you can't want me after telling me this!"

"You have a lot to learn, my dear." Rede's voice was mocking. "And you won't deny that, having bought the merchandise honestly, I'm surely entitled to confirm my possession of it?"

OTHER
Harlequin Romances
by JANE ARBOR

Pact without Desire

by

JANE ARBOR

Harlequin Books

TORONTO·LONDON·NEW YORK·AMSTERDAM
SYDNEY·HAMBURG·PARIS·STOCKHOLM

Original hardcover edition published in 1979
by Mills & Boon Limited

ISBN 0-373-02299-9

Harlequin edition published December 1979

Printed in U.S.A.

CHAPTER ONE

FOR Sara the hour-long freedom to leave the air-
craft and walk the concourse at Bahrain gave her
her first glimpse of the East, and she was experienc-
ing it alone. Her luggage had gone aboard labelled
'Mrs Rede Forrest', her new passport named her as
'Sara Forrest'; for a week now she had signed herself so, and the narrow gold ring guarded by her
engagement diamond signalled her as the married
woman which, so far, she was not.

So far ... But even if Rede—his name still came
strangely—had not had to fly out on a crisis call from
Singapore on the very afternoon of their wedding-
day, would her marriage have been more real than
in name only even yet?

She did not know. Since that traumatic evening
when she had accepted his bizarre proposal, she and
Rede had been on no terms of intimacy from which
she could sense his intentions of their future. They
had met on most days, had lunched and dined and
shopped for clothes for her at his dictation. At the
end of his leave, after their wedding, they were to
fly together to Singapore—but that plan had been
disrupted by his urgent departure ahead of her.

The hours she had spent with him, nervously
feeling her way to knowing him, had had a dream-

like quality of their happenings being not quite real, and only when she was alone had she come down to the earth of questioning where a marriage with so little romantic heart to it could lead, and why they had contracted it.

Rede had claimed that he wouldn't be the loser by it, but where was his gain? She wasn't wealthy, she hadn't aristocratic standing, and as in the circumstances he couldn't have married her in order to cherish her—*why*? And even of herself she only knew a confusion of motives which baffled her.

Revenge against the man—Rede Forrest—whose influence with Cliff Iden had virtually taken Cliff from her? Yes, there had been a brief temptation to tie him to a loveless marriage to pay him out for that. But the meanness of that rancour had passed. Pride then? The chance Rede's proposal had given her to carry out her reckless threat she had made to him—that, now hating Cliff for his betrayal of her, she would marry the first man who asked her? Yes, that still perhaps, but by no means uppermost. For there had been something else ... something she could only define as an acute awareness of the magnetic importance of Rede to her life.

She didn't love him—of the stranger who had cynically taken her at her word and proposed a loveless marriage to her, that was impossible. But still her world, empty of his dominant direction of it, would now, she suspected, be empty indeed; the time before she knew him appearing flat and featureless as a desert. On too short an acquaintance to justify it, he had become foremost in her thoughts, and against all reason or prudence she had begun to feel committed to the bloodless pact with which he had claimed her. She had to see it through. (But 'through' to—where?) She had no answer to that.

The in-transit passengers were being recalled to the plane, and, pursued by Arab souvenir-vendors to the last, she joined the queue for yet another security check. Singapore was several flying hours away. If she were lucky and could be left alone by the diligent cabin staff, she might catch some sleep. For Rede would probably be meeting her, and from her short knowledge of his standards she sensed that he would expect reasonable chic after even a seventeen-hour flight. She mustn't arrive looking like a rag.

But Rede did not meet her. When the porter she had managed to corral had collected her bags from the carousel and loaded them on a trolley she was hailed by name from the barrier by a beaming Malay in faultless chauffeur's uniform. In English which was good though stilted, he took her over from the porter and, apologising for the distance, conducted her to a long grey open car in the car park, where she chose to sit in the passenger seat beside him.

'Tuan Forrest unavoidably detained in office,' he explained. 'But he send flowers for you, mem,' he added with a backward jerk of his head at the back seat. Sara looked round at the big sheaf in florists' wrappings which would have greeted her if she had sat there. 'I see. Thank you,' she said, and forced her feeling of let-down to bow to 'unavoidably'.

The car slid smoothly along tree-lined streets and avenues basking in late afternoon sunshine, flanked by luxurious hotels and shopping precincts and peopled glamorously to Western eyes. The chauffeur ('call me Lim, mem,') treated Sara to a running commentary as he drove.

'Singapura beautiful city, mem. Great seaport— fourth in the world. Many lovely sights—the Jade House, the Orchid Gardens, fine temples, Sentosa Island. A happy city too—work and good housing and schools for all—you will see.'

The drive was a long one, mostly through residential areas, leaving the central business district largely to seaward. But when, Lim said, they were within ten minutes of Rede's house in Nassim Road, he proposed to make a detour to show Sara the Temasik building. (Tuan Forrest's orders, if Mem were not too tired.)

He pulled up at the wrought-iron gates to a long, one-storeyed building standing back in a courtyard of ornamental flowerbeds. It was white and gleaming, with sun-canopies to every window and upward-turned eaves to its Oriental roof.

Sara mentally compared it with the soot-begrimed London offices of Temasik to which Cliff had sometimes taken her when they were engaged. So this was Rede's kingdom, named Temasik for the island's ancient title of 'sea town', the source of all the jade, silks, batik, pewterware, porcelains and silver which went out from here all over the world. She thanked Lim for showing her the place and gave him a description of its opposite number in London, at which he shook his head in shocked disbelief.

After his offices, Rede's luxurious house was no surprise. It was one of a few mansions in its exclusive avenue, behind walls hung with bougainvillea and morning glory; white too, with flowers climbing over trellis on its walls, and a first-floor carved balcony running its length. Sara's pulse quickened at the sight of it. Was this the place—because of Rede—which she was going to have to call 'home'?

At the door Rede's houseman, Chakan, took her bags from Lim, and Buppa, Chakan's wife and Rede's housekeeper, welcomed her into the cool hall, spread with rugs and sweet with flower scents.

Hands in a prayer-attitude beneath her chin, Buppa bobbed. 'Madam would like to go to her suite, no doubt?' Madam smiled that she would, and followed the woman up a wide curving staircase to a big sunny room overlooking sloping lawns. The bed was a fourposter; a door gave on to a bathroom, another door opened briefly by Buppa showed Rede's bedroom; both rooms shared a window balcony.

Sara asked what time Rede might be home. Buppa was vague. Soon perhaps, or not yet. Evening—some time. For dinner—yes, surely. He should be told Madam had arrived. In the meantime Madam would like tea to be brought to her, and then to rest?

The tea, fragrant with lemon, was brought by a
tiny child in a maid's smock, who volunteered her
name as Malee and her age as seventeen while she
turned down the bed-coverings and drew linen
blinds against the sun. When she had gone, smiling
and bobbing her way out, Sara sipped the tea grate-
fully, then took a silk wrap from her overnight bag,
unzipped her sleeveless linen dress and lay down
on the bed. But not to sleep, for all her lack of rest
on the plane. She was too keyed-up, too chillingly
apprehensive of Rede's homecoming to find her
here. She had perhaps an hour—less?—more?—in
which to wait for him, and she had to brace herself to the ordeal of meeting him for the first time
since their marriage and parting three hours later.
Her thoughts went back to the first time she had
ever seen him ...

The usher at Cliff's wedding had met her halfway
up the aisle. 'Friend of the bride—or of the groom?'
he asked in a church whisper.

'Neither,' she told him, and had obeyed the shoo-
ing motion with which he intimated that the place
of mere spectators was further back. She joined a
pewful of people who shuffled closer to make room
for her, glancing briefly at her immediate neighbour, and glancing again while his profile was
turned to her.

Seated, he was head and shoulders taller than she.
He was dark, tanned, almost to swarthiness; she had
an impression of a high-bridged nose and a strongly

jutting chin; he was dressed as informally as she was, and when he interrupted her scrutiny by looking her way there was a glint of conspiratorial amusement in the dark grey eyes he had turned upon her.

'Like me, having no wedding-garments, you've been cast into the outer darkness? You're not a guest?' he had enquired, not whispering, but only for her hearing.

Her sore spirit had been in no mood for badinage.

'No,' she had replied shortly, facing front.

'Then you collect fashionable weddings, perhaps?'

'*Collect* them?'

'As some people collect stamps or Old Masters. On "Weddings I have Known" you are possibly a connoisseur?'

'I'm not snooping for the sake of it. I—happen to know the bridegroom, that's all,' and, suddenly roused by the man's impertinent curiosity, she had turned on him. 'Since you're so interested as to why I'm here, what about you?' she had demanded.

'I? Oh, I—happen to know both the bride and the groom.' His hesitancy mimicked her own.

She had put studied insolence in the glance which appraised his open-necked shirt, patterned silk cravat and beige slacks. 'But they didn't invite you as a guest?' she had insinuated.

'I didn't know I could attend. I only flew in from the Far East this morning, noted the date, remembered the name of this church and stopped by——'

He checked as the soft meanderings of the organ voluntary had ceased, signalling the imminent appearance of the bride—Cliff's bride, passing up the aisle in a rustle of silk and chiffon to meet Cliff, expectant and nervously smiling at the altar, while Sara had stared unseeingly at the Order of Service sheet in her hands.

'Dearly beloved, we are gathered together ...' There at Cliff's side, in the place of the stranger named Isabel Carbery, should she, Sara Duncan, have stood some time in the near future, hearing the lovely age-old words spoken over her and Cliff, making her vows to him, accepting the promised faith of his.

Before he had gone out to Singapore for his three months' trial for his new job with his firm, Temasik, exporters of luxury wares from the East, everything had been in accord. He and Sara were to marry soon after his return, and a fortnight before it she had given up her post as a television studio assistant, in order to tackle the delicious task of preparing a trousseau for young wifehood in the tropics. And then Cliff had come to her with his craven confession.

At first he had been lonely in Singapore. Then there had been this lovely girl, Isabel, out from England on a visit to her Singapore-based relatives; herself the daughter of a director of the English branch of Temasik; Cliff's introduction to her made and his courtship encouraged, by his chief-to-be, the Overseas Director, Rede Forrest. So would Sara free him?

She had done so, feeling no charity towards him, indulging the savage hope that he might be eaten by remorse. Meanwhile, *he* had his Isabel. It had been she, Sara, for whom there had been only emptiness ahead. She hadn't even a job any longer, would have to start again.

Now she was remembering how, unable to watch him marry Isabel Carbery, she had kept her eyes lowered until the tears of self-pity threatened to course down her cheeks. Then she had flung back her head, lest people should notice ... her curious neighbour not above asking why she was not following a ceremony she had presumably come to see. But in the instant of trying to behave like everyone else, she had realised the culpable folly of having come, pretending to an excusable need for a last sight of Cliff and a first sight of the girl who had supplanted her.

For primarily she had come in order to rub salt into her wounds by indulging her near-hatred of Cliff—and suddenly to be cherishing in church only the sour rancour of her hatred and jealousy—had appeared to her like sacrilege. She couldn't, mustn't stay. She had to get out, and had plunged into the aisle, reckless of the turned eyes watching her go.

There had followed three dreary weeks of seeking a new job—the daily task of going for interviews or calling at the agency to see what had 'come in'. She could have returned to her former job, but refused to face the humiliation of admitting her broken engagement. She hadn't gone near the studios since she had resigned, leaving her late colleagues to conclude that she had had a 'relatives only' wedding and had gone straight out to the East with Cliff.

Relatives only—that had been an ironic laugh in itself. For she had none nearer than an aunt in the North and some cousins. The small ground-floor flat, one of several such warrens in a formerly one-family mansion in Wimbledon, had been her home since she had been able to afford to leave the hostel where she had lived when she had first gone to London. Her name had been in the slot below her own bell at the front door. But only friends and tradesmen ever rang for her. No one of her own at all.

Then there had been the day which she was to remember as That Evening. Earlier its rain, no spring shower but a dance of hailstones on the ground and a fusillade upon window panes, had soaked her while she was out, and when she came in she had bathed, changed into a kaftan and tied her hair back carelessly with a ribbon, not bothering again with lipstick. When the time came she need only exchange the kaftan for her nightgown and she would be ready for bed. She had gone through the same routine on the day of Cliff's wedding and this time she had found in the pocket of the kaftan's skirt a thick fold of paper.

She had taken it out, uncreased it, the silver

engraved Order of Service which she had brought away with her. She scanned it. Wagner ... Mendelssohn ... Bach Toccata and Fugue ... Love Divine, All Loves Excelling ... Cliff and Isabel would have gone out to Singapore by then, and as she crumpled the sheet and had thrown it in the wastepaper basket, she had thought again of the man, her pew-neighbour, who had offered it to her, noticing she hadn't collected one at the church door.

That man. Rede. Her husband—The man who, when she had had to answer her bell a moment or two later had stood at the outer door, his bare head and his shoulders the immediate target of the over-flow from the porch roof, and to whom her instinc-tively hospitable, 'Oh—please come in,' had been exactly simultaneous with her startled recognition of him—'that man'.

At her impulsive invitation he was inside the hall and almost inside her living-room, which had no vestibule. She had stared at him, her heart thump-ing. How had he found her? *Why*?

He had murmured a perfunctory 'May I?' fol-lowing her into her room, where he held out his hand to her. 'Sara Duncan?' he had questioned, as if knowing he would not be corrected, and added, 'Rede Forrest', in the same flat tone.

Rede Forrest! The Overseas Director of Tema-sik, who had fostered and encouraged Cliff's match with Isabel Carbery, when Cliff must surely have told him he was already engaged! Along with her contempt of Cliff, she had despised a Rede Forrest she was never likely to meet. But had met—in church at Cliff's wedding. With a hand at her throat she had demanded of him, 'What do you want? And how did you find me?'

He had turned a palm upward. 'Simple. On the afternoon we met I invited myself belatedly to the wedding reception and described you to the bridegroom.'

'*Described* me to Cliff? How?'

She could still remember how hotly her colour had flooded at his analytical scrutiny of her carelessly tied hair, the informality of the kaftan, down to her bare feet in mules. (Had she been aware of his magnetism even then?) He said, 'Physically? I'll have to remember—Yes, I told him you were young, twenty perhaps, not much more; that you had this centre parting to your hair held back with combs; that you were healthily honey-coloured with an upstage profile—which was about all you kept turned to me—that you were medium tall and walked with a swing from your hips, as all women should.' He had paused. 'I could have added that, on a cursory judgment, you seemed to curve in all the right places, but it wasn't necessary—Iden recognised you and was suitably embarrassed.'

'How do you mean—"suitably"?' she had demanded.

'Seeing that he was embarrassed, I made him tell me why, and got the story of his break with you before I let him go.'

'And got my name and address too. As if it were

any business of yours!'

'Call it interest, rather. Haven't you ever wanted to add another scene to a real-life one you've witnessed? There was a pretty girl, weeping at a wedding to which she hadn't been invited——'

'I *wasn't* crying!'

'Near enough to it that you had to leave the church, lest it should be noticed. I could have followed you, of course. But what would you have thought of me if I had?'

'That, because I'd let you speak to me in church, you thought I was easy game for a pick-up. But where's the difference in your going to Cliff? You've followed me up just the same!'

'Added the missing scene, let's say. Not noticeably to Iden's credit, but——'

'Nor to yours, Mr Rede Forrest, if I may say so,' Sara remembered having cut in. 'I can't believe Cliff wouldn't have told you he was engaged to a girl back here when you began to push him into marrying Isabel Carbery. Well, didn't he?'

'He called it a minor entanglement and made nothing of it, and as I was concerned to have him married, I didn't press the point. Temasik prefers married men on its Far East staff.'

'As Cliff would have been—to me—if you'd left him alone. But why?'

Rede Forrest had contemplated a corner of the ceiling above her head. 'The Malaysian women are very beautiful. Seductive too, to a degree, and marriage makes for a certain stability,' he remarked.

'Oh—!' Again she knew she had blushed. 'You're saying you don't want your staff tempted to take mistresses. Are *you* married?' she had shot at him.

'Not yet. I'm the exception that has proved the rule,' he had said, and then, 'Isn't it time you rewarded my concern by giving me your version of your broken engagement?'

'You know it all. You had it from Cliff.'

'But only a sneak view of *your* reaction—of your weeping for him in church.'

She had turned on him then. 'Just how obtuse can you get?' she had demanded of him. 'I've told you I wasn't crying for love of Cliff. It was from anger with him, and scorn at myself for having believed in him, and hatred for—for anyone who'd encouraged him to think I didn't matter——'

'Meaning me, I suppose?'

'If you like. If the cap fits.' She had raged on, 'And what's more, I was so angry then and since that I've been ready to vow I'd marry the first man who asked me, just to *show* him. To show him!' She had concluded wildly, oblivious of her hearer until he had said quietly, 'And supposing some "first man" held you to that?'

She had laughed bitterly. 'No problem. Men have an instinct about jilts and they steer clear.'

'So that, in asking you to marry me, I *am* your "first man"?'

She had stared at him, open-mouthed. 'How dare you make a mean joke like that? You must know I wasn't serious!'

'And I am. You vowed it, you said, and I'm justified in taking you at your word. You want to "show"
Iden, you claim, and I'm affording you the chance
to do just that.'

'Which I'd have to be mad to accept!'

'Not so mad that you aren't intrigued by my asking. And you realise, don't you, that in Singapore,
as my wife, and with Iden already there, you'd be in
the only position available to you just now to carry
out your threat? Stay in England, and you have
none, and where's the point of thumbing a long
nose at your victim if he isn't there to suffer your
doing it?'

Sara had known she shouldn't have listened, but
later she knew that the insinuation of that question
had been the turning point of her resolve. From
having no doubt that she was adamant against his
assumption that she would accept his offer of marriage from so low a motive, she had come round
to letting him persuade her that to show herself
to Cliff as the proud survivor of his rejection of her
was good reason enough to accept him. Tempted
and a little dizzy, she had heard herself asking at
last,

'You—you'd marry me in cold blood—just like
that?'

He had agreed tersely, 'Just like that. But don't
think me merely quixotic. I find myself with a use
for marriage now.'

'To—to just anyone?'

'I'm offering it to someone with enough motive

of her own for accepting—a vengeance she needs to get out of her system,' he had said, and it had been too late for the sanity of refusing him when he slid down her finger the ring—a single diamond in a chased gold setting—which his assurance had brought with him. She had allowed him to commit her. She had committed herself.

Beyond the drawn blinds the sky had darkened. Sara hadn't noticed its happening and couldn't understand why, until a glance at her watch showed that more than an hour had also passed without her knowing it. That meant that, rigidly awake as she had felt, she must have fallen asleep after all. She had not unpacked, nor done anything to make herself presentable to Rede when he came home. But she had only just swung her legs off the bed when she saw the door from his room opening very quietly, and she lay back quickly, pulling up the silk coverlet again.

Rede came in and over to the bed. His hair was brushed back wetly, he was newly shaven and he wore only a knee-length robe. She had never before seen him not fully clothed; he had never yet seen her in only a slip, and the implications of this 'first time' sent a constriction chokingly into her throat.

She swallowed upon it. 'I——'

His voice clashed with hers. 'You were asleep when I came in earlier. I'm sorry I couldn't meet you, but I was too tied up. Lim would have explained?' He looked about the room. 'You got my flowers?'

'Yes. I left them downstairs for your man to arrange. They were lovely—thank you. I hadn't thought I was tired enough to sleep. Is it always as dark as this by seven o'clock?' (Talking for the sake of postponing having to say or to listen to anything more intimate, she thought.)

Rede said, 'It isn't really dark. It's the heat which builds up storm conditions by early evening at this time of year. You'll learn to be prepared for rain before nightfall on a good many days.' He sat down easily on the bed, and she drew aside her feet to make room for him. He half-turned to face her; one hand on the far side of her knees supported him, the fingers of the other plucked at the hem of the coverlet, turning it slightly back. 'You really weren't tired by the journey?' he asked.

'Not *by* it. During it, yes. There were so many comings and goings and interruptions. I'm sure they were all meant for my comfort, but I'd have given a lot to be left more alone,' she said.

He did not reply to that. She watched the veins start on the back of his hand at its increased pressure on the yielding bed until, knowing his eyes were intently upon her, she raised her own to meet his, darkly searching her face while his free hand at her back lifted her towards him. He said, 'Well— wife?' And then, 'Marriage-wise, we're behind on time, aren't we? The present will have to catch up——'

Marriage-wise! With the phrase he had answered the question she had posed to herself at Bahrain and before and since. He meant to take her, as a man would take his bride for love on their wedding-night; to take her—if not now, sooner or later—in a travesty of a physical union sweet with fulfilment, in the name of the loveless bargain he had struck with her—her surrender to him implicit in its terms.

Fair was fair, was no doubt how he saw it. In return for her as yet undefined use to him—his name, his protection, his support for her already almost forgotten revenge on Cliff—he probably saw the scales of the transaction well weighted in her favour and meant to even things up by demanding and taking as of right the male prerogatives which marriage gave him.

She shrank within his hold, feeling herself almost physically dwindle in contrast with the overplus of his strength and size. If he tried to force her, she couldn't fight him. But even short of compulsion, how could she endure the false caresses to which he would expect response; how yield to him without shuddering under a touch and an intimacy which he couldn't pretend meant any more to him than to her?

It was going to be now, she realised, when he shifted position to lie beside her, to align his body to the length of hers and to seek her lips.

Surprisingly, his kisses there were gentle as they were exploratory on throat and eyelids and temples, and though she could not answer kiss for kiss as if he were her lover, she felt her resistance lessen. Until, when he slipped a finger beneath the ribbon of each strap of her slip, baring her shoulders to the hollow of her breast, she thought in sudden revulsion, *He is expert at this. He knows all the moves. How many shy, reluctant women before me has he schooled in this way, step by gentle step, towards the compliance he wants?*—and she thrust away from him, panting and biting her lips.

To judge by his frown, he neither accepted his rejection nor understood it. He said, 'You knew I should come to you. You were waiting.'

She shook her head. 'No. I meant to unpack and bath and change, but I just lay down for a little while and fell asleep.'

'With no plans for seeing me until you were clothed and in your right mind?'

'You hadn't met me at the airport. You weren't here. I didn't know—I didn't expect——'

'—That I'd want to rectify the omissions of our wedding-day as soon as I could? Come, you're no green girl; you were on the point of marrying Iden, and not without recognising the graces and favours to be given and taken in marriage, I should hope?'

'But ours wasn't an ordinary marriage. It was—— It's called "of convenience",' she objected.

'And, taking the world as a whole, very little less common than the other kind, I'd say. We Westerners are in the minority in demanding romance. And you surely don't suggest that all the arranged marriages of civilisation and of history are and have been strictly celibate?'

She sighed emptily. 'I don't know. I only know about ours—that neither of us claimed it was for love, and——'

Rede cut in, 'Not "and". "But". Agreed that neither of us claimed it was for love, *but* for all that it's going to be marriage in every other known sense of the word, and so'—his fingers bit deeply into the soft flesh of her arm—'are you a willing partner to its consummation or not?'

Sara cried out in panic, 'You can't force me! It would be——'

He put a forefinger to her closed lips. 'Don't say it,' he admonished. 'It's an ugly word, and it needn't apply if——' He broke off and drew her close again, holding her with one arm while his other hand wandered in search of warmth and softness and the signs of a quivering response.

At first she lay rigidly, without protest or welcome to him. But slowly her senses awoke to a physical pleasure at his gentle, undemanding touch; pleasure as sweet as the stroking of a kitten's silky head or her nostrils taking the fragrance of a rose. The pleasure lasted, and from being at attention at her sides, her arms went round him, feeling the hardness of the muscles there and the ripple of tanned skin on his shoulder-blades. And then, somehow, the pleasure changed to an urgency of need, and she came alive in the arms of the body which had now abandoned gentleness for mastery, titillation for possession.

She was drowning ... she was being drawn towards the sun of his passion ... she was crumbling, crumbling away in utter surrender and into a dreaminess of content when at last his savage claiming of her was over.

She lay at his side for a long time after she could tell from his even breathing that he had fallen asleep. Then she slipped from the bed, and when she came back from her bathroom he had still not waked. She stood looking at him, vulnerable in sleep, her feelings a conflict between a gratitude for his pleasuring of her and a resentment of his assurance that their union was a foregone conclusion in a marriage which had pretended to no love or tenderness on either side.

Again she questioned his motives in marrying her so casually. He had claimed to be above his Company's ruling on marriage, so why had he fallen into line now? And even though he had, he could have complied with the letter of the law by making her mistress of his house without asking any deeper relationship of her. But that, she supposed, had to be his need and power of dominance which she had sensed very early and which had her usually in thrall to his will. Which was strange. She had never regarded herself as biddable, but biddable she had been to him so far, even in a surrender which she knew he would ask of her again as his right.

Very quietly she had taken a change of clothes and her make-up case from her luggage, and with her back to the bed at her dressing-table she did not realise Rede had wakened until he was standing behind her, his hands on her shoulders, looking at her reflection in the dresssing-mirror. As their eyes met, she was trembling a little. But his question was practical, matter-of-fact. 'Would you prefer to dine at home, or to go out?' he asked.

She stopped trembling. 'I think your housekeeper expected you in to dinner,' she said.

He shrugged. 'She's used to my changing my mind if I care to, and you'd probably like to have your first night on the town. Here you can eat Chinese, Indian, European, Indonesian—there are nearly as many cuisines as there are days of the week. I suggest we eat Thai seafood at the Lotus Room. I'll ring for a table for nine o'clock,' he said, and when he had used the telephone on the bedside table, he went back to his own room.

Sara thought, If he'd kissed me, or said something kind or even laughed with me, I'd have been able to hope it was going to be all right. But after *that*—to discuss nothing but where to take me to dinner, I might be nothing but a call-girl he'd engaged for the evening! The phrase Bed and Board occurred to her. That was what she had bought with her agreement to marry him—Bed and Board. She had forgotten completely the temptation with which he had wooed her—the chance to triumph over Cliff, and very soon after she had accepted Rede, it hadn't been very important, nor counted enough for her to recall it now.

What did matter now was the unknowable future with Rede—strangers still, both of them.

CHAPTER TWO

BEFORE she had decided what to wear for the evening Rede came back into her room and she consulted him.

He suggested a gold lamé gown, as narrow as a tube from neck to ankle, with a high mandarin collar and an encrusting of beadwork giving epaulette width to the shoulders, which he had chosen for her himself in an Indian shop off Bond Street.

Sara demurred, 'For a restaurant meal?'

'For the Lotus Room it won't be too dressy,' he said. 'And on our first night out you have to do me credit.'

She did her best, using more elaborate make-up than she would have chosen in England, adding drop earrings and putting up her hair in a looped style drawn into a heavy knot. Standing before the mirror she hardly knew herself; fair though she was, she had gone exotic in a big way!

There was a surprise in store when she went down

to meet Rede in the hall, where he helped her into her wrap, saying, 'I thought we wouldn't take the car. I sent Chakan to fetch a trishaw instead and he has it at the door. You'll never have ridden in one, I daresay?'

They went out into the silken warmth of a night from which all the storm threat had passed, leaving the navy blue sky pricked by a dazzle of stars. Chakan stood by the tricycle carriage, ready to help her into it; the rider-driver balanced impassively on his saddle, one foot on the ground, moving off smoothly when Rede joined her, sitting thigh to thigh with her on the made-for-two seat.

'It's today's version of the rickshaw,' Rede explained. 'The rickshaw man used to run in the shafts; his grandson takes it easy on a saddle.'

'Easy work—toting two adults along?' Sara questioned.

'Oh, they're well geared and they see that they're well paid, and for the passengers, with the hood up, the thing can be as intimate and romantic as a hansom cab. Or so the tourists seem to find them. The trishaw stands are always busy,' he said carelessly.

The Lotus Room, he told her when they reached it, was an old manor house turned restaurant. It served Thai food in Thai fashion on low candlelit tables, decorated with bowls of floating water-lilies and orchids; the patron's choice of dishes was arranged crescent-wise around his place, and he helped himself from them in turn, taking his soup last.

Later in the evening there would be a floor-show of dancing by the girls and men of one of the Eastern Culture schools of the city.

Sara asked Rede to order for her and she savoured all her dishes with interest when they came, deciding on a snap judgment that, of her prawns and noodles and spiced oysters and vegetarian curry, the accompanying sauces were all. Sweet or piquant or lemon-fresh, they made everything attractive, different, mouth-watering to a degree. She was acutely aware of Rede's watchful eye upon her, amused and, she hoped, gratified by her enthusiasm for everything strange. Though she drank only the light white wine he had ordered, Wimbledon and cold rain and crowded Tube trains seemed very far away, in another world.

The candles cast dark shadows; one's neighbours at the next nearest table weren't to be seen very clearly and people walking about the room were largely in silhouette. Which was probably why Sara did not realise what was happening until Rede stood, the inclination of his head acknowledging a man and a woman who had approached their table.

She looked up—and froze. The man was Cliff in a tropical dinner-suit, the woman in a flowered silk gown Sara had last seen at an altar with him. She was russet-haired with a creamy skin; her arm was tucked possessively into Cliff's; she was looking at Sara with interest but with none of the blank surprise on his face. He was staring at Sara as Robinson Crusoe might have stared at Man Friday, as if she were not quite real, or a being from another planet. After the first dismayed flutter of her heart at the sight of him, she schooled herself to meet his gaze without flinching. And on a chill flash of intuition questioned silently, *Was this a chance meeting? Or did Rede expect them to be here?*

Rede was saying easily, 'Ah, Iden—you and Sara know each other, don't you? Isabel, meet Sara, my wife. Sara darling—Isabel Iden, an old friend before she married. You'll be seeing quite a bit of each other, I daresay. Socially speaking, we move in rather a small orbit, and we tend to clan.' He added to Cliff, 'We're staying for Sara to see the dancing. Will you join us for coffee, or haven't you had dinner yet?'

Cliff said, 'No, we're just on our way to our table.' To Sara he said with stiff hesitancy, 'This is a— tremendous surprise,' while his wife sent him a look of perplexed annoyance before managing a thin smile for Sara.

She said with false gaiety, 'I suppose I've got to accept that Cliff would have known heaps of girls before he met me—too bad for him, isn't it, if you're part of his dark past catching up with him here!' Then she accused Rede, 'You and Cliff have been keeping secrets from me. He'd told me he'd heard you'd married while you were over in England, but not that he knew who your fiancée was.' Her full lips formed a moue. 'I'm hurt—with both of you. But especially with you, Rede. Considering the good friends we've been, and that you've been back here more than a week now, you could have confided in me. Yes, I'm hurt, I really am.'

'Don't be,' he advised. 'And not with Cliff, who's known no more than I allowed the grapevine to publish—that I'd come back married. To whom? Well, I confess I wanted Sara to burst on our restricted society like a meteor, and I'm sure Cliff, for one, would agree that as the perfect English beauty, she does impress! Mm, Iden? I've won myself a prize?'

At Cliff's embarrassed murmur of, 'I've always known Sara has all that it takes,' Sara blushed inwardly—for Cliff, for Isabel, for herself, and not least for Rede's sadism. He's enjoying this, she thought fiercely. He's playing cat-and-mouse with us all, and she was never more thankful than when Isabel, with another smile devoid of warmth for Rede and for herself, urged Cliff on their way.

Sara laid aside her napkin and picked up her bag. 'Do you mind if we leave now?' she asked Rede.

'Leave?' he echoed. 'I brought you out for the evening, and you haven't had it yet.'

'I've had enough.' She turned on him 'You *knew*,' she accused.

'Knew?'

'That Cliff and his wife would be dining here tonight, and you intended we should meet!'

'I gave you the choice to dine at home.'

'But if I'd wanted to, you would have dissuaded me. You *meant* to come here.'

Rede shrugged. 'Why deny it? In the office this morning Iden mentioned that, as it's Isabel's birthday, he was bringing her here to dinner, and it seemed too good an opportunity to allow you to miss.'

'Of meeting him face to face, on my very first day, with his wife looking on—*an opportunity?* Rede, how cruel can you get?' Sara appealed.

He disclaimed, 'Nothing further from my thoughts. Cruel to whom, may I ask?'

'To Cliff, to Isabel, to—to me.'

'By offering you the earliest possible chance to achieve the one ambition with which you married me—the first man to ask you and to put you in the way of the triumph you'd promised yourself—cruel?' he taunted.

'More than—because you were enjoying the spectacle. You could have told Cliff before this that we'd married, but you chose to shock him in front of Isabel, and you impaled me like a moth you'd caught—claiming you think I'm beautiful which I'm not, and inviting Cliff to admire my—my points, as if you were both judges at a Miss World beauty contest. Why did you do it? *Why?*' she pleaded.

'Mainly because, in the matter of nose-thumbing at your ex-fiancé and your rival, you didn't appear to be doing much for yourself. You may have thought you were "showing" Iden the door and flaunting your capture of a husband at Isabel, but no one would have guessed it. You didn't utter a word, and after all I've done to bring about your avowed dearest wish, you disappoint me, wife, you do indeed! I judged you better capable of sustaining a thirst for vengeance than that, d'you know?'

The malice she read into the bantering words enraged Sara. 'If by "all you've done" you include your having asked me to marry you, then all I can say is that I wish you never had!' she declared, and saw Rede's expression change—frighteningly—as his fingers clamped round her wrist beneath the cover of the table.

'Say that again—and mean it,' he muttered in a tone of threat. '*Say it again!*'

She couldn't. With his eyes holding hers in unspoken but dreaded ultimatum, she couldn't bring herself to it. 'You heard. I've said it once,' she replied, weakly giving in to the unknown.

'And about as recklessly, let's hope, as you've made empty, self-martyred declarations before,' he retorted and, as she made to rise, used leverage upon her wrist to press her back into her chair. 'Where are you going?' he demanded.

'Home. Back to the—your house.'

He shook his head very slowly. 'Oh no. When we leave, we go together—and not yet. Watching the classical dances of the East is a favourite relaxation with me, and you must learn to enjoy them too.' He released her wrist. A waiter sprang forward to turn their chairs to face the curtained dais at the end of the room. Rede took out his cigar-case. 'May I?' he asked, opening it. Sara nodded her dumb permission for him to smoke.

She was prepared merely to endure the rest of the evening, but she was soon fascinated by the colour and magic of the scene on the stage. Most of the dances told a story in mime—of the unrequited love of a hideous monkey for a lovely girl; of gallants to the rescue of maidens menaced by dragons; of heroes warring for the favours of gods; of Cinderella themes and of rivals in love.

The decor was subdued—in deliberate contrast to the colour and flamboyance of the costumes, to the extravagance of headdresses, the metallic sheen of armour and brandished swords, and the incredible beauty of the women dancers, all graceful, speaking movement from literally their supple fingertips to the sway and undulations of their slim bodies. Without a word being spoken, each tale was told to its conclusion in scenes of pure theatre.

Sara watched entranced, drawn into another world while the spectacle lasted, and when it was over and Rede took her arm to guide her out, she was still so much in legendland that the memory of their acrimony at dinner returned with a shock. Rede called a taxi for their journey back and allowed her to sit as far from him as the cab would allow.

'You enjoyed that?' he asked.

'It was out of this world,' she said on a sigh of pleasure. 'The colour, the acting! Are they all professionals, the dancers?'

'Possibly only one or two we saw tonight are full professionals, but the dance is so much a part of the culture out here that the children are trained to it from babyhood, and it's so lofty an ambition with them that the girls in particular will take on almost any job by day in order to be taken for training in the dance schools at night, with the occasional professional engagement as prize.'

'They were all very beautiful,' said Sara.

'You noticed that?'

'Yes——' She checked, remembering his oblique hint of his reason for having sponsored Cliff's marriage and, embarrassed by it still, she hoped he wouldn't refer to it again.

He didn't. He sat across from her in silence, and by the light of the street lamps which flashed intermittently into the darkness of the cab, she glanced at him covertly—the stranger she had married, whose direction of her dominated her will, to whose assertion of his right to make love to her her body's need had utterly surrendered in passion tonight, yet who, an hour or two later, had deliberately pilloried her and been ruthless with her rebellion.

Supposing she had defied him and had repeated her wild regret at having married him? What would his reaction have been? She didn't know and shuddered to guess—and not only because she feared his contempt, but because his withdrawal from her would matter to her; matter too much.

She couldn't, could *not* go through the motions of marriage at his side, without there being some rapport between them—something that would give the lie to the cold calculation of his proposal and of her bemused acceptance of him. On some plane or other they had to meet. But where?

At the house Buppa had left a tray of drinks in the hall, but Sara refused anything, saying she would like to go straight to her room. Rede said, 'I'll take a nightcap before I go up,' and bade her goodnight with a light kiss upon her cheek, leaving a desert of unspoken things between them.

She prepared for bed slowly, listening and hoping. If he came to her, she would try to express some of her thoughts in the cab—that, having married, they had to make it work, that she would do her best; that even if they did not love, they could tolerate and learn—mentally she rehearsed her conciliatory approach to him, imagined his response.

But he did not come.

The maid Malee brought Sara's continental breakfast to her room the next morning at nearer ten o'clock than nine, far later than Sara wanted to rise, but hadn't asked Rede when he would expect to see her. Tuan hadn't wanted Mem disturbed earlier, Malee said, but he would come to see her before he left for the office, if that suited Mem's plans.

Sara wondered what plans of her own he thought she could already have in this house, this city, this country, all new to her. More likely, she thought, that Malee's tact had edited Rede's message, and that such plans as there might be would be his, for her to carry out.

And so it proved. When he came, he bent across the bed to kiss her with as little feeling as he had kissed her goodnight. Then he said, 'I shan't be around all day, but I'm asking a friend to call and take you out and put you in the picture as far as she can. Her name is Belmont, Ina Belmont. She's a widow, and has been a Singapore fixture for years. She goes everywhere and knows everyone—a walking gossip-column, in fact. But as you won't be able to avoid knowing her sooner or later, you may as well begin at once. She'll be taking you out to lunch, then around the city wherever she thinks best.'

'Oh,' said Sara to this programme. 'That will be kind of her, but does it have to be today?'

'Why not today?'

'Well, oughtn't I to get to know your staff; learn about the running of the house and all that?'

Rede's gesture was impatient. 'It's run very satisfactorily ever since I've owned it, and I daresay it will survive for as long as you need to look about you further afield. In any case, when I married you, I didn't see you in the role of a *hausfrau*—all domestic chores and penny-pinching. What makes you think I did?'

Sara said unhappily, 'I don't know *how* you saw me. You never told me.'

'No? Well, primarily as a wife.' He paused. 'As I thought I made you understand when we met again last evening. If not, I'll furnish as many more lessons as you like—a pleasure, I assure you!'

'Rede, don't, please!' she protested in agony. 'Don't sneer at me, at—at our relationship. We both took it on, and I didn't deny you—I didn't cheat. You didn't have to force me, and I didn't think you ever meant to, and I was grateful. Please believe that!'

'Grateful? For what?' he questioned.

'To you—for being gentle with me and for pretending enough to save my face that you weren't taking me merely as a duty you felt you owed me as—your wife in name.'

He laughed at that, and she looked at him, hurt. But the laugh had softened his expression, and from where he had walked over to the window, he came back to stand by the bed. He said indulgently, 'Evidently I'm further ahead of you than I thought. For don't you know that a man can rarely "pretend" to make passionate love to a woman for the sake of saving her pride or whatever? He either can or he can't. It's as basic a fact of nature as that.'

'But he can make love without loving,' Sara said forlornly.

Rede shrugged and turned away. 'True. But that's another thing again, and when you married me for your own purposes, I don't remember that you made loving and being loved a condition of the deal?'

She stared at his back. 'Of course not! I hadn't the right——'

'Correction. It never entered your head to ask it. Any more than it entered mine that in accepting me, you could possibly imagine I had plans for a life of celibacy for both of us. In my view marriage means what it says—which I've already demonstrated, and intend to.'

As if that ended the argument, he moved towards the door, but Sara couldn't let him go without making the effort she had planned overnight. She appealed, 'Rede, I'm sorry I exploded last night. Because if you really thought I couldn't wait to confront Cliff with my marriage to you, I suppose you were justified in doing what you did.'

He turned to face her briefly before he left. 'Making excuses for me? Don't bother,' he advised. 'If it had the desired result, I congratulate you an on inspired revenge, and as a spectacle alone, it was worth my trouble.'

'A—a *spectacle*?' But her outraged echo spoke to empty space.

In spite of his advice, when Sara went downstairs she went to the kitchen quarters to make Buppa's better acquaintance and to ask about marketing and menus and the domestic routine of the house. Both Buppa and Chakan seemed gratified by her interest, but she sensed Buppa's reluctance to hand over any reins. Buppa said, 'Mem doesn't need to bother her head,' too often for Sara's encouragement to play mistress of the house, and she saw that her acceptance in that role would call for some tact on her part. But how was she going to fill her time, if she hadn't Rede's backing for her running of his home?

Mrs Belmont rang up to say she would be calling at about noon, and Sara was putting in time in the garden, waiting for her, when Malee came to say she was wanted again on the telephone.

'Mr Forrest?' Sara enquired.

'No, mem. Mr Iden his name, he says.'

Cliff? For her? Ringing here? Sara heard her voice rough with dismay as she answered, 'Sara, Sara Forrest here. Yes?'

Cliff said urgently, 'Sara? You are alone? I've got to see you. Where and when can you meet me today?'

'I can't,' she said flatly.

'Why not? You must. I can't come to the house!'

'Obviously. But a Mrs Belmont is coming to take me out to lunch and to show me the city. I'm expecting her any minute now.'

'Ina Belmont? That busybody! But you still must make time to see me.'

'Why?'

'Because—damn it, you must know why, Sara. After last night—I've got to know how and why you've arrived here, married to Rede Forrest. For can't you imagine what it did to Isabel, finding we knew each other? She gave me hell later, and she's still thirsting for blood if I don't explain—why I was shocked, which I was, and who you are, and what we were to each other.'

Sara said coldly. 'Well, I'm afraid that's your problem. I've enough of my own.'

'What do you mean by that?'

'Nothing. Anyway, I can't meet you. That's final.'

'You must. Please, Sara. I've got to have something reassuring to tell Isabel. You know the Raffles Hotel?'

'No, why should I? I only flew in yesterday.'

'I meant you must have heard of it. It's a landmark, and any taxi-driver can bring you to it. I shall be there at three, and I shall expect you.'

'Don't,' said Sara, 'I shan't be there,' and rang off as Malee showed in an elderly woman with greying blonde hair, prominent blue eyes and a skin weathered to a map of wrinkles. She came to Sara, announced, 'I'm Ina Belmont. Call me Ina, everyone does,' kissed Sara on both cheeks, then held her off at arm's length. 'So you are Sara, Rede's bride, and a *peach*. He is a fox, keeping you under wraps until now, never bringing you out here while you must have been engaged. But better late than never. You'll be a wow with the men, if Rede will let them near you. Anyway, what would you like me to show you? Fond of flowers? Antiquities? Objets d'art?' Without waiting for Sara's choice, she decided on a visit to the botanical gardens to see the orchids and the lotus flowers, and then to the Jade House, a mansion housing a private collection of priceless jade and porcelain.

She was a lively, talkative companion, relating her life story of Army service in India under the Raj, of losing her colonel husband twenty years earlier and of her settling for good in Singapore—'the East, the only place for a woman when her blood is turning thin, my dear.' She whisked Sara at speed along sun-dappled avenues, past fabulous flower-displays where Sara would like to have lingered, and 'did' the jade collection with the surefire expertise of a tourist guide. She said Rede had suggested they should lunch at the Singapura Hilton, adding ingenuously, 'It'll go on Rede's account, dear, so don't be mean with yourself if you want to choose the most expensive thing on the menu.'

Sara found her amusing, if slightly exhausting. Clearly her interest was mainly in people and their affairs. She name-dropped shamelessly and treated Sara to potted biographies of as many of Rede's friends as she forecast Sara would be meeting. After lunch they went window-shopping in the city's luxury stores and then for a drive along leafy Queen Elizabeth Walk with its magnificent view over the harbour.

'I shall take you to tea at the Raffles Hotel,' Ina announced, and at Sara's involuntary start, asked, '*Not* the Raffles? Why not?'

'Sorry—I didn't mean No.' Sara had taken a swift glance at her watch to see that the hour was long past three, so there was no danger that Cliff would still be there. 'I'd like that,' she added. 'It's quite famous, isn't it?'

'Straight out of Kipling and Somerset Maugham, dear. Like Shepheard's in Cairo and Reid's in Madeira. Out of its generation now with all these multi-storey jobs crowding it. But it's the *only* place where you can get cucumber sandwiches and Earl

Grey tea, à la Ritz—too utterly nostalgic, I assure
you,' Ina enthused.

She left Sara to enter the foyer while she parked
the car. Straight out of the dazzling sunlight into
the dim cool interior, Sara had difficulty in focus-
ing her eyes, and as she stood waiting to do so, a
hand gripped hers frenetically and the figure between her and the reception desk proved to be Cliff's.

'You came! I waited on, half hoping—' he
breathed, but she interrupted him.

'I didn't—that is, not to meet you. Mrs Belmont
brought me here for tea, and she'll be with me in
a minute. So please——'

'Well, well!' It was Ina breaking in, all smiles.
'You two know each other already? Fast work,
young Iden, considering that Rede's Sara only
arrived last night. And how is *your* lady wife?'

'Very well, thank you. And I knew Sara in England,' Cliff muttered.

'You did?' Ina's bulbous eyes gleamed with interest. 'So there's a coincidence—you meet again!
And you'll have tea with us, boy—yes?'

But Cliff excused himself. He had business, seeing a buyer, and couldn't wait. 'See you soon. We
must have a party,' Ina speeded him on his way,
and during tea probed Sara for details which Sara
did her best to evade.

Ina mused, 'You may imagine how tickled we
all were when your friend Cliff Iden and Isabel Carbery fell for each other after Rede had introduced
them, considering how long Isabel had been setting

her sights at Rede himself!'

Sara caught her breath. 'How long?' she echoed, recalling that last night she hadn't understood Rede's speaking of Isabel as 'an old friend'. 'But I thought Isabel Iden was only on a visit here with friends or relatives when Cliff first met her?'

'On a visit of several,' Ina corrected. 'She'd been coming out for at least the last five years in the spring, and there were those of us who quite thought she and Rede might make a match of it. But apparently there was nothing doing.'

'I see,' said Sara, mentally filing information which she hadn't heard from Rede, and Ina went on, 'Something of a beauty, Isabel, isn't she? You've met her, of course?'

'Not until last night at the Lotus Room. She and Cliff were dining there, and so were Rede and I.'

'Then it was only Cliff Iden you knew in England?'

'Yes.'

'Ah——' Ina nodded sagely, as if doing some mental filing of her own.

She drove Sara home in the early evening, saying, as Sara thanked her and they parted, that they must 'do this again quite soon', and that she had meant what she had said to Cliff—she would lay on a party for Sara. An evening party on Sentosa Island would be fun ...

Rede came home shortly after Sara. He suggested they dine at home, and had Chakan bring drinks to their balcony. After dinner Sara might like to sample the offerings on television, and meanwhile he wanted to hear about her day.

She told him, editing her slight recoil from her escort's exuberance, only for him to laugh and agree, 'Heart of gold, and all that, Ina. But a little of her goes a long way, you found?'

'A bit,' she admitted. 'Not that she wasn't kindness itself, but I would rather like to buy a map and explore the city on my own—bit by bit, slowly, not all at a tourist gulp. And on foot, quite often.'

Rede said, 'Not used to this climate, you'd find footwork pretty trying. When I've got the car, Lim could take you in the runabout anywhere you want to go.'

'But I think he likes to sell the sights of the city too,' she objected. 'Couldn't I set out on foot and pick up a trishaw when I got tired—or lost?'

'Or take a trishaw or taxi from here. We always use the same men, and Chakan would call one of them for you.' Rede set down his glass and rose. 'When I'm at home, I usually eat at about eight. Will that suit you?' he asked.

Sara said it would, and that she would like to bath beforehand. After he had gone she wondered whether it would always be like this for them—polite, tolerant strangers on the everyday plane, on any other, wary enemies or lovers only at their bodies' compulsion, nothing more. Guiltily she wished she could have been frank with him about Cliff's invitation and about Ina Belmont's gossip as to his long friendship with Isabel, but fearing his reaction to both, she had said nothing. And while she was afraid of him and he despised her, how far could they hope to get?

After dinner he watched television with her, choosing programmes he thought she would like, advising her of trash she would not. A pleasant, domestic evening for two people who were worlds apart.

Three days later, after a similar quiet evening, Sara was about to go to bed, when Rede said, 'Just a minute—I'd be obliged if you'd tell me what your date with Iden at the Raffles the other day was in aid of? I believe you had one?'

Sara caught her breath. 'You're mistaken. I had none,' she denied.

'Oh, come! You met him there. I ran into Ina at the Yacht Club yesterday. She said she'd thought she would have to introduce you to each other, but from her hearing him say to you, "You came", she supposed he had expected you. But when she asked him to have tea with you, he wouldn't. Ina didn't make that up?'

'No,' Sara admitted. 'It did happen like that. He was in the foyer of the hotel when we arrived.'

'You didn't mention it when you told me about your day's foray with Ina.'

'It wasn't important. It was a chance meeting, that's all.'

'A mere coincidence? When the ploy he was out on that day was a batch of calls on silver merchants in Chinatown? And his call to you here that morning? You don't deny he made one?'

At bay, like a cornered animal, she protested, 'Yes, he did ring me here, asking me to meet him, but——'

'You didn't mention that either.'

'Did I have to, when I refused to see him? Or must I conclude that anything I do or anywhere I go is going to be reported to you? If that's so, you should have warned me you keep spies on your staff and among your friends, you really should!' Sara raged.

Rede said icily, 'Calm down. No spies. As mere a couple of chances as Iden's keeping a date which you say you refused him. You'll learn in time that Ina's curiosity about her friends is as 'satiable as the Elephant's Child's, and her total recall of anything that interests her is that of a computer. But entirely innocent. She's never malicious, but we're all grist to her mill of absorbing news and passing it on. On the staff of the *Straits Times* she could have worked up to Editor any time she liked. As for the other chance—Expecting a call from the mainland and asking about it when I came home that evening, I was told there had been only two local calls, both for you. That was so?'

Sara nodded. 'From Mrs Belmont, and from Cliff.'

'That's what I heard from Malee, that she'd asked for his name to take to you. He wanted a date which you say you didn't give him, but why did he want it?'

'I didn't give him time to tell me, except that

he and his wife were both shocked by the way you'd thrust me at them at the Lotus Room, and he wanted to know why.'

'Why appeal to you, rather than to me?'

'I don't know. Perhaps because you're his chief, and——'

'——Or because the exercise worked a little too well; we dazzled him with you, and he's having regrets at having let you go? You'd be flattered by that, I daresay?'

Sara flared, 'You know I wouldn't! I've finished with him. And if I'd been flattered, should I have refused to see him?'

'Caution might have warned you against it. After all, he has a wife, and you are mine. But if you were firm with him, that's as well. For, from the safely entrenched position of marriage, you might have found having him as a scalp for your belt not unattractive, perhaps?'

'You'd suspect me of playing him off against you for—for kicks?'

'Let's say, for justifiable lack of loyalty to the rather bizarre terms of our contract, you could feel?' Rede offered.

Her head went up proudly. 'I shall honour them,' she said.

'Meaning you'll make the best of them. Handsome deal—of a proposition I may say I expected you to turn down flat!'

She stared, open-mouthed. 'But you made it! You proposed to me! And when I did refuse, you

argued, you made me listen, you persuaded me——'
With fingers at her trembling lips, she faltered,
'You're saying——? Saying you didn't *want* me to
accept? You hoped I wouldn't?' In a flash of intui-
tion, 'You'd have thought more of me if I'd said
No?'

He nodded. 'If you'd said "Go to hell" or words to
that effect, and meant them, I'd have respected that.'

'Then why didn't you take back your proposal?'

'I'd made it, and as I told you, marriage was in
my programme at the time.'

'To—to anyone? Any handy girl would have
done?'

'I had proposed to *you*.'

'And married me, despising me—Oh!' At the
confirmation of her fears Sara turned away, drained
of all hope for the future. 'I'm going to bed,' she
muttered. 'I can't——'

'I'll come with you.'

'Please, Rede, no——!'

But she had hesitated long enough for him to
join her at the door. Upstairs, he followed her into
her room and turning to her, took her into his
arms. She leaned back within his hold and looked
up at him. 'Rede, you can't want me after—all
this!'

'All which?'

'Of accusing me of deceiving you, trying to catch
me out. And the rest—your contempt of me, your
using me! Please——' She attempted to twist free,
but he held her fast.

He mocked, 'Your immaturity has still a lot to learn, my dear. For instance, that bouts of ex-changed home-truths are commonplaces of most marriages, and whether he's bested in them or not, a man can quite enjoy asserting himself in—other ways. Or put it like this—the true gourmet appre-ciates the spice of a quarrel as a vinaigrette sauce——' Ignoring her shudder of distaste at the unnecessary metaphor, he went on,

'What's more, you won't deny that, having bought the merchandise honestly, I'm entitled to confirm my possession of it from time to time? Come.'

As he spoke he spread the wide neck of her dress down over her shoulders, and with her upper arms thus pinioned, he took her hand and led her over to the bed.

And presently the skilled gentleness was there for her again, and the pleasure, betraying her to the hot tide of passion which engulfed her as be-fore.

CHAPTER THREE

STILL awake long after midnight, Sara relived her body's rapturous surrender to Rede's claim to it, and suffered an after-shame which eclipsed the brief de-light she had known under his spell, and that of her own urgency to give and to take, while she could forget that he made no pretence of loving mere merchandise that he had bought. More than that, his frank admissions tonight underlined his low opinion of her.

Though what cause had she for hurt? her honesty questioned. When she had married him, it had not been for love as she had once known it for Cliff—basking in his admiration of her looks, the days of their meetings always red-letter, their quarrels distressing, their reconciliations sweet, the longing to be his all, for which another name was jealousy. That had been love. How much or how little of those feelings applied to Rede now?

On their first occasion together after he had made their marriage a reality, he had expected her to do him credit, and she guessed that in the matter of dress and poise, that challenge would hold. Waiting to see him, encountering him, was pulse-quickening too—a kind of small adventure every time. Reconciliations? They had had none—only a temporary eclipse of their differences at Rede's insistence on his marital rights. But—jealousy? With a sense of shock she realised that already she could be jealous about him; jealous of his past, of his now and of a future in which he might possess another woman—loving her.

Yes, jealousy told its tale. *'I've begun to fall in love with Rede.'* Her whisper tested for hope, but foresaw only the despair of knowing that the next time he made love to her without loving her, it would be her heart as well as her body which his detachment would humiliate. And to think that if she had said No to his cynical proposal of marriage, she would have kept her self-respect and his! (Worth it—at the expense of never seeing him again?) Though her conscience answered Yes to that, her need to love and be loved answered No.

Meanwhile the everyday of a life that was not without its novel pleasures had to go on. For instance, there was the bliss of planning out-of-doors ploys with reasonable certainty of sun and warmth. True, the island did stage its capricious storms from time to time, but the evening rains were short-lived, carrying no threat over to the dawn of the next beautiful day.

Sara bought her map; walked, rode the network of the bus services, took trishaws into Chinatown, boarded junks for tours of the harbour, experienced the peace and silence of dedicated temples, spent hours in the city's flower-parks, and learned her new world with enthusiastic curiosity.

For the most part she enjoyed it independently of Rede, but they dined out once or twice a week, where she savoured or rejected every strange dish of every regional menu which was put before her. She learned to use chopsticks, conformed with back-to-front meals where the soup was served last, and doffed her shoes for taking tea from cushions on the floor in a Japanese *tatami* room.

She could not resist the exotic fruits which had never reached the English shops—durians and chikus and mangosteens and the melon's tropical cousin, the papaya. She longed to experiment with some of the foods and sauces which she found particularly attractive, but found Buppa not too receptive to the idea of sharing her kitchen. Sara, who had hoped to make her debut there as mistress of Rede's house, was disappointed. At first she thought she had an alternative plan, until that was vetoed by Rede himself.

On her earliest explorations of the house and gardens, she had been attracted by a single-storeyed annexe to the main house which, though it was fully furnished and its kitchen equipped, seemed to have no immediate purpose. Asked about it, Buppa said it was a guest-lodge, and Rede confirmed that some of Temasik's Asian clients on business trips preferred to stay there instead of being put up in the house or in hotels.

'They're very family-conscious, and when they bring their wives along, they like to keep to their own customs of cooking and eating, which they can do in the cottage undisturbed,' he added. 'And this year it's going to be occupied more or less permanently fairly soon.'

'And I couldn't use the kitchen meanwhile?' Sara asked.

'To play at cookery? If you must, Buppa shall make room for you in her kitchen and help you,' he promised.

'She won't like that,' Sara warned.

'A great many people may not "like" my orders, but they find it best to carry them out,' was his crisp retort, typical of his autocracy and which left her feeling snubbed. That he had spoken to Buppa was clear when that lady offered the use of the kitchen to Sara's trials and errors, and when she realised how very amateur were Sara's efforts, she even offered help and advice. Sara did not lay claim to the cottage again.

Cliff had not tried to see her, and she concluded he had been able to convince Isabel that he, Sara and Rede were not in league against her. Neither he nor Isabel were present at a drinks party which Rede gave at the Temasik offices to introduce Sara to some of his colleagues, and when Sara remarked on their absence, he replied with a caustic, 'Sorry to have cheated you of a second chance to lay on your act, but it wasn't an occasion for the junior staff,' which Sara let pass without comment.

She was able to tell herself she had imagined Isabel's thinly veiled hostility at their first meeting until, on her coming home one afternoon, Malee told her Isabel had called and had chosen to wait in the garden to see her.

Isabel, protecting her creamy skin from the sun in the shade of a cedar, refused the tea which Sara offered. Greeting Sara with a limp handshake, she came at once to the point of her visit, and it wasn't a social call.

'I came to see you because I think I'm entitled to your version of what you and Cliff were to each other before he met me. *He* says you were just one of several girls he'd been dating in England, but that doesn't explain his double-take at the sight of

you at the Lotus Room, and I don't believe him,'
she said.

Sara could not resist murmuring, 'What a pity,
to feel you can't believe your husband.'

'Well, can I?' Isabel pressed.

'I don't know. He may have had other girls, but
before he came out here the first time, we were
engaged.'

Isabel claimed, 'I knew it, or something like it.
He wouldn't admit you meant anything to him, but
now he'll have to. He should have realised I could
get the truth from you.'

'Though is it worth while making trouble about
it, now that it's all over?' questioned Sara.

Isabel's eyes narrowed. 'But is it? How can I be
sure of that?'

'On my side, you can be quite sure,' Sara assured
her.

'On his, though? The way he looked at you——!
And it was you he telephoned the next morning,
wasn't it?' Isabel added, with an air of having kept
this long shot in reserve.

'He did ring, yes,' Sara admitted. 'But how did
you know?'

'We've an extension in our bedroom, and I'd just
picked up the receiver there when I heard him tell
someone he "must" see him or her. He flicked the
switch then, cutting me off, and as we were hardly
speaking after the Lotus Room scene, I didn't ask
him about it. But where did you meet him that day,
and what did he want?'

'I didn't meet him. I refused,' said Sara.

'Why?'

'I had nothing to say to him, nor wanted to hear anything from him.'

'Or could be—you were afraid *your* new husband would find out you'd kept a date with Cliff?' Isabel speculated shrewdly.

'Rede knows that Cliff telephoned and that I didn't meet him.'

'On sure ground there, are you? Though couldn't he still think Cliff's wanting a date rather odd? Especially considering how soon he caught you on the rebound from Cliff? And Cliff has never told me to this day that Rede Forrest knew you before he went on vacation to England this time.'

'He didn't,' said Sara. 'We met at your wedding.'

Isabel stared. 'You weren't *at* my wedding to Cliff!'

'Officially, no. Neither was Rede.'

'You gatecrashed it? I know Rede came to the reception.'

'I didn't. I was only at the church.'

'To see Cliff married to me? Poor you!' There was scant pity in Isabel's tone. 'And yet'—knitting her brows in calculation—'only a matter of weeks later you turn up here, married to Rede. If you were upset over Cliff, pretty fast work, that? For your sake, not shotgun, I hope?'

Colouring hotly at the insolence, Sara resorted to sarcasm. 'Perhaps that remains to be seen. I daresay you have a calendar and can add?' she insinuated, knowing that the retort would increase Isabel's hostility, but unable to resist making it.

Without apparent contrition, Isabel said 'Sorry' and rose to leave. But she had another shot to fire. She said, 'I daresay Rede wasn't a bit sorry we met at the Lotus Room that night. He could have been looking forward to flaunting his new bride at me. Though I daresay he hasn't told you that every year I've been out here on vacation he's dogged me like my shadow?'

Sara said calmly, 'No. All I heard from Cliff was that Rede introduced you and gave his blessing to your marriage.'

'Yes, well,' Isabel shrugged, 'making the best of losing out to Cliff, of course. But I did rather suspect he wouldn't have told you. Makes things rather awkward for us all round, doesn't it? You and Cliff, Rede and I—really, an onlooker couldn't be blamed for suspecting the men to be up to a bit of wife-swapping, could he?'

Sara did not reply and let her go on this exit-line. Her last salvo had confirmed Ina Belmont's gossip, but Sara made herself deny its rankling. Mere gossip and Isabel's own boasting of conquest— need they add up to threat? She wouldn't let them!

Ina Belmont had made no empty promise of giving a party on Sentosa Island, once a fortress, now being developed as an exclusive resort. Ina issued her invitations for an evening affair—swimming in the lagoon, a barbecue supper on the beach and danc-

ing at the golf club-house until the last ferry left
for Singapore.

'Do we go?' Sara asked Rede, passing Ina's card
to him.

He glanced at the date. 'I can't. You do,' he said.

'Why not you?'

'I'm flying to Rangoon on business the day before, and I shall be away overnight. But you'd like
to go, wouldn't you?'

'Alone?'

'You can go with Ina, or Lim can drive you to
the ferry and you can join the crowd there. You'll
have met a good many of the people Ina will have
asked, so you needn't be alone for long.'

'I'd rather be going with you to Rangoon. I suppose I couldn't?' Sara ventured.

Rede shook his head. 'Strictly stag, I'm afraid.
An only-just-in-the-balance advantageous deal for
teak, and none of us are taking along feminine dis-
tractions. Another time, another trip perhaps. Not
this.'

Dressing for a party which included swimming,
a picnic and indoor dancing offered problems. Sara
chose a ballet-length dress of emerald Thai silk with
a matching knotted kerchief for her head, wore
flatties on bare feet and put high-heeled strapped
sandals into her beach-bag with her swimsuit. Lim
drove her to the ferry-stage where, as Rede had pre-
dicted, other people she knew were going over at
the same time. They were fortunate in the weather.
There had been no rain that day; the air was still

and warm, and the sun, a glowing ball of fire, had gone down from a cloudless sky, now a great arch of darkness above Sentosa's woods and landscaped parks and palm-fringed white sands.

After a time in the water Sara did a lazy crawl-stroke away from her group, then turned to float, blissful and relaxed in a silence broken only by the distant chatter of the people on shore. She allowed her thoughts to fantasise—she was happy, she had no problems; Rede, flying unexpectedly from Rangoon, would come to find her; they would swim side by side, he would be kind and under-standing, and afterwards——

There was a beat of limbs disturbing the silk of the water behind her. Someone was following her up and it was not Rede. It was Cliff. He trod water beside her and when she turned over and began to swim shorewards, he turned with her.

'I saw you strike out away from the others,' he said.

Pointedly, 'Yes, I wanted to be alone. Where is Isabel?' she asked.

'Helping Ina at the barbecue. Rede isn't with you?'

'No, he's away.' From the shallows Sara paddled over to where she had left her towel and bag, but when she sat down to dry her feet and legs, Cliff came to sit beside her.

'Please, Sara—this is the first chance I've had! Or rather, the first I've dared to take——'

'To say what?' she put in coldly.

'To ask about Forrest, of course. How it all happened about him. He'd asked me who you were at my wedding, but I never thought he was serious about gett'ng to know you, and now Isabel has convinced herself you only married him to spite me, and came out here to make trouble for her. But that's not so, is it? You had little enough time for it, but you and Rede did fall for each other in a big way? You are in love with him, Sara?'

Sara burned her boats. 'Yes,' she said.

Cliff sighed with apparent relief. 'And from the way he showed you off to us, I'd say there's not much doubt about *him*. But Isabel believes I still hanker a bit for you, and that you'd like to have me as well as Rede, as a kind of fringe benefit.'

'Not any more. Or she shouldn't,' said Sara.

'What do you mean—not any more?' Cliff queried.

'I've told her myself that I've finished with you; that she has nothing to fear from me.'

'Oh——!' To Sara's wry amusement he looked almost offended by the bluntness of that. He added with a shrug, 'Well, that's the way it goes, I suppose. Though perhaps Isabel is right, and you didn't take long about putting Forrest in my place.'

The conceit of men! thought Sara. 'Give or take a day or two, just about as long, I daresay, as it took you to put Isabel Carbery in *my* place,' she told him with the quiet assurance of having had the last word. She stood then, picked up her bag and would have moved away. But he stopped her with a hand on her arm.

'Fair enough,' he said. 'But there's something else with Isabel. She's restless and disappointed with my job at Temasik, and she thinks you've persuaded Rede to keep me down.'

Sara scoffed, 'That's absurd! I've no influence with Rede at all in the firm. Anyway, you've been out here only about three months.'

'That's what I tell her—that it's early days yet,' Cliff agreed. 'But she maintains that you'll see I never get kicked upstairs at Temasik, and she's doing her best to push me into joining a chap we've met, George Merlin, an orchid exporter in a big way. He's here tonight. I'd like you to meet him, so if you stick around at the barbecue I'll introduce him to you, if I may?'

'If you like,' Sara agreed indifferently. But he stopped her as she turned away once more.

'Nothing of all this to Rede, of course, Sara?' he urged.

She gave him her promise with a brief nod.

Ina Belmont was a born hostess, keeping, it seemed, a dozen eyes open to see that the food was ready on time, that all her guests were served and that no one was left without a companion or two for more than a few minutes. In fact it was she who brought George Merlin to Sara, along with one of her cooking aides bringing the miracle of a *bombe surprise* dessert for both of them.

George Merlin was something of a puzzle. His brushed-back hair was iron grey, but he had the body and easy movements of a much younger man, was handsome if, as Sara didn't, you liked the male model type, and he spoke with a very faint accent which she could not trace.

Spooning admirably firm ice-cream from beneath its blanket of warm meringue, 'How is it done?' he asked Sara.

'I think speed is the answer,' she told him. 'You slam meringue over the ice-cream and shoot it into and out of a hot oven before the ice-cream realises it's supposed to melt. And then you serve it pronto before it can.'

He nodded. 'I see. I must get Katin, my cook, to try it,' he said, and then, 'Won't you tell me about yourself? Though of course I know already that you're the lovely young wife Rede Forrest brought back from his last trip to England. And so?'

Apart from that, and that she was fascinated with Singapore, there seemed little enough to tell him about herself, and she turned a similar question to him. 'You export orchids, a friend tells me,' she said.

'A friend?'

'Cliff Iden.'

'Ah, Cliff. Yes, we send them all over the world, with Thailand our only rivals in the size of business we do. If you're interested, you should let me show them to you, growing, some time. May I do that?' he asked.

'I'd like that.'

'Then quite soon? Tomorrow even? It's some

way upcountry from the city. Do you drive a car?'

'No, but——'

'Then I'll call for you at about noon and we'll lunch. Unless you're engaged in the morning, and would rather make it later?'

But Sara said No, she would prefer the morning, as she was expecting Rede home in time for dinner. For a moment she had hesitated about accepting the invitation, but she had no other plans for the day and Rede couldn't mind her being driven into the country to see a wealth of orchids growing in the mass.

Ina was as efficient in shepherding her guests into the lounge and bar of the golf clubhouse and persuading them to dance as she had been in organising their supper out of doors. Sara danced a few times and talked with people she knew. She was not in Isabel's neighbourhood at all, and Cliff only cornered her briefly on the return ferry.

'Isabel didn't want to meet you, but I saw you'd corralled George Merlin under your own steam,' he said.

'Ina introduced us,' Sara corrected.

'Oh well, as long as you've met him—but don't let on to Rede that I'm putting out feelers in his direction, will you?'

'I thought I'd already promised you that,' she said.

George Merlin drove north out of the city along the Bukit Timah road, and far sooner than Sara thought

there was open enough country for orchid plantations he turned up a drive leading to a white bungalow facing a swimming pool across a wide patio
bordered by flower beds.

'Welcome to my house,' he said as he stopped
the car.

Surprised, Sara said, 'Oh——! I thought we were
going out to your orchid fields?'

He looked concerned. 'Did I give you that impression?'

'I thought so.'

'I'm sorry. I meant to show you my private display of some of the rarer varieties which I grow
here in my gardens. I should have made myself
more clear—I export orchids, I don't raise them
on a commercial scale. That's done on farms over
on the mainland, too far inland to have taken you
today. No, we'll have lunch, if Katin has done her
stuff, and I'll show you the garden afterwards. You
would like a drink out here on the patio?'

Sara got out of the car, disappointed and more
than half convinced she hadn't misunderstood his
promise, but that she had been misled. He left her
to go into the house, where he summoned someone
by clapping his hands and speaking in Malay. She
wondered about his wife, but his possessive 'my
cook', 'my house' suggested he was a bachelor. Katin
was the only woman's name he had mentioned, and
she, following him back on to the patio carrying a
tray of drinks, was a young Malay girl.

She was short and plump, with her race's raven

hair cut in a short bob and a fringe above her eyes, beady as jet buttons. She wore a Western mini-dress of scarlet cotton, flaunting generous bare thighs and legs the colour of black coffee. She had no smile in answer to Sara's as she put down the tray with a clumsy thump, and then set up and laid another table with three place-settings. After a brief 'Meet Katin', without introducing Sara to her, her employer ignored her and talked to Sara until she returned with three covered soup-bowls and, to Sara's surprise, sat down at table with them.

She said nothing. As if she were not present George Merlin explained, 'Katin can speak English, but only when she chooses,' and a few minutes later addressed her in Malay, apparently complaining of the soup. It was certainly tepid and tasted like cab-bage-water, but Sara was acutely embarrassed when Katin flushed darkly, snatched up all three bowls and flounced back into the house with them. They did not return, the soup reheated. Instead a dish of rice and tough veal fillets arrived, to be served by Katin with a defiant clatter of implements which to Sara's ears said, 'Take that and like it—or else!'

But there was further bewilderment in store for her when, after the deplorable meal, Katin brought coffee. As she passed his cup to him George Mer-lin put an arm round her at about the level of her brief skirt and drew her to him. She leaned against him, simpering, until he said something teasingly, when she frowned, tossed her head and marched away.

George Merlin laughed. 'If she has a fault, my
little Katin, it's that she's appallingly jealous,' he
remarked.

'Jealous?'

'Of any woman within range. In this instance, of
you.'

'But——? Well, I thought you said she was your
cook?' Sara questioned.

'And housekeeper, in which office she's slightly
less competent than as a cook. But as what might
be called companion of the bedchamber, she's——!'
He broke off and set the fingers of both hands to
their thumbs in a gesture expressing excellence.

Sara blushed. 'I'm sorry. I didn't understand,'
she muttered.

He said quickly, 'I've embarrassed you. But why?
You're not so naïve, surely, that you're shocked?'

'I am—surprised.'

'You should congratulate me, rather, on the iso-
lation here which makes for discretion in itself. Men
in the city in the same situation are forced to keep
a wife or a hag of a chaperon as a cover-up to allay
the talk of their friends. Very hampering, that. I
count myself lucky.'

'Do you *know* any men in the same situation?'
Sara challenged him.

He shrugged his despair of her. 'Oh, my dear,
really! You can't be *that* ingénue!' He broke off to
listen to the sound of a motorised bicycle ticking
over, and a minute or two later Katin spun down
the drive and out of sight. 'Katin, registering high

dudgeon in the usual manner,' he commented easily. 'She goes back to her village to cry on the shoulder of one of her many relatives, and depending on how much she decides I should be punished for entertaining you, she may or may not return tonight.'

'She—sleeps here?'

'Of course.'

Sara had had enough. She stood up. 'May I go to see the orchids now, Mr Merlin? After that, perhaps you'll drive me back?'

'With pleasure.'

Certainly his display of orchids rivalled any that she had seen. It ranged through all the colours of the spectrum and innumerable shapes of blossom. Sara lingered for nearly an hour, expressing wonder and admiration, though when she asked her host if he chose and cultivated them personally, he disclaimed responsibility.

'I employ experts,' he said. 'So I expect near-perfection, and am content, as in my admiration of other forms of beauty, to regard myself merely as a connoisseur.'

As he spoke, his bold glance over her figure pointed his meaning and did the same again when they returned to the patio and he said, 'I'd suggest we use the pool before you go, if I'd thought to ask you to bring a swimsuit, or if anything of Katin's chubby measurements would fit anyone as slender as you.'

Disliking the innuendo and deciding that a little of George Merlin's suavity went a very long way with her, Sara declined hastily, 'No. You're kind to think of it, but I really must go. May we now?'

But he demurred, 'Ah—well, that makes for difficulty, I'm afraid. As Katin has deserted, and I'm expecting a man to call on business, I ought not to leave until he comes. Once he does, I can despatch him quite quickly. But a little while longer, do you mind?'

Annoyed though she was, there was nothing Sara could say, and they sat talking desultorily while, as time spun out, her patience did likewise. Once she ventured, 'Perhaps I could catch a bus?' But it seemed there was no bus route within miles. 'Call a taxi from the city, then?' Not necessary at all. By now his colleague was bound to be on his way.

Sara refused tea but accepted an iced mandarin juice. In passing the glass, his hand went over hers and pressed it. He said, 'I wonder that your husband shouldn't have taken you to Rangoon with him. So soon to leave his young bride for a night—for shame!'

Sara gazed fixedly into the amber-gold in her glass. 'Rede is on a business trip with other men,' she said. 'He couldn't take me.'

'Even at the risk of leaving you to the mercies of wolves like me?'

She lifted her eyes and looked straight at him. 'You're very frank, Mr Merlin. *Are* you a wolf?' she asked.

He laughed cynically. 'My dear, we all are at the sight of prey we fancy, and given the opportunity to hunt it down!' He added as if upon reflection, 'Even a husband suffering grass-widowerhood for one night in Rangoon could find himself tempted,' to the nastiness of which Sara could not trust herself to reply, and the grotesque situation of being forced to sit there beside him went on.

It was at the point when she had decided for certain that the expected caller was a myth and the delay a ruse to keep her, that a car sounded in the drive and her companion managed an 'Ah, here's my friend at last,' with a satisfaction which did not ring true.

There was no reason why it should have done, for the car drawing up was no stranger's. It was Rede's, and it was Rede who crossed the patio his face a study in pent annoyance. He nodded briefly to George Merlin and answered Sara's exclamation of his name with, 'We closed the deal more easily than I expected, so I caught an early plane.' He turned to her host. 'You will excuse my wife now? I'd like to take her home.'

George Merlin said easily, 'Of course, and though I'm sorry to be frustrated in taking her myself, thank you for loaning her to me for the day.'

He followed them to the car and bade Sara a suggestive au revoir. With one hand on the steering-wheel and the other closing the door on his side with a bang, Rede demanded, 'And what did that crack mean? *Are* you going to see him again?'

'Of course not,' she denied. 'I don't think he can

help being pseudo-gallant. But I found him quite odious.'

Rede glanced quickly her way. 'Unexpected perception. But how come you let yourself get involved?'

'How did you know where I was?' she countered.

'When I got home and found you were out, I rang Ina to see if you were with her. She said that, as you were both on your own at her party, she had introduced Merlin to you and he'd told her later that he was taking you out to lunch.'

'On a tour of his orchid plantations was what *I* thought,' Sara corrected. 'But he pretended I'd misunderstood him; that he'd only meant to show me the orchid specimens in his garden and for luncheon, tête-à-tête. Or not tête-à-tête, as it turned out,' she added. 'His cook came too. But she took umbrage when he grumbled about the food, and later she rode off somewhere on a moped, leaving us together.'

'His cook or his current mistress?' questioned Rede.

Sara started. 'What do you mean? How did you know?'

'How did *you* know?'

'He admitted it, or rather, he boasted about it and about his freedom to do as he liked out here.'

'And so—a liar and a womaniser, and you stay with him all afternoon in cosy chat! What was next on the programme? Dinner and a stay overnight? As a matter of interest, when *did* you mean to leave, if I hadn't come along?'

Rede's tone had edged, putting her on the defensive. 'When he was willing to take me. But he kept on making excuses, knowing, I suppose, that there was no other way I could go.'

'You could have slapped his face and walked out on him.'

'Walked—more than fifteen miles into the city? Besides, there was nothing—specific—to slap his face for. He'd only looked and—and hinted with a kind of leer. Oh, Rede——' she appealed, 'you've got to believe I couldn't stand the man, and that I was never so thankful in my life than when I saw your car drive in!'

'With me at the wheel? Or would Lim have done as well?'

'You, of course.'

'I'd have thought one knight-errant was as good as another. But next time, switch on your intuition radar a bit earlier for a type like Merlin, and meanwhile I'll have a trenchant thing or two to say to Ina on the company she keeps,' Rede said, then changed the subject completely.

'The Classical Dancers of Thailand are at the National Theatre tonight. Would you care to go?'

'Lovely,' she agreed. 'What time?'

'Curtain up at eight. We'll have supper at the Hilton afterwards. Dress up.'

This was Rede, keeping her at the arm's length of their pact, admitting nothing of whatever concern for her had taken him out to George Merlin's place in search of her. She would have liked to believe that jealousy had brought him, the same need of possession which she had towards him—which was impossible to hope. But he *had* returned from Rangoon earlier than he need have done; he *had* accepted her recoil from that repulsive man; he *did* want her company on their evenings out. And there *were* times when her body must have attraction for him ...

Crumbs. Probably only self-deceptive crumbs at that. But there was comfort to be had in collecting them and hoping they told the truth.

That evening, at Rede's side, enjoying his pleasure equally with her own, she was as nearly happy as she had been yet.

CHAPTER FOUR

THE fanciful euphoria of that evening was to be disturbed by the news which Rede had for her a few days later. When he joined her in the garden for their pre-dinner drink, he told her,

'I'd like you to have Buppa do what's necessary in the cottage for a guest who'll be arriving tomorrow night, flying in from Kota Tingii on the mainland by the afternoon plane.'

Sara asked, 'Oh—the businessman you said might be coming semi-permanently?'

'Not a man. A woman. Or rather, a young Malaysian girl, my protegée while she attends the Dramatic Culture School in Queenstown as a dance student.'

'Your protegée?' Sara looked her surprise. 'You haven't mentioned her before?'

'She's only arisen as a problem during the last few months and I've only recently decided on this arrangement for her.'

'To live by herself in the cottage? How old is she, then?'

'Doubtful. She must be eighteen; she could be a little more. She was abandoned by her parents who were probably killed in the Communist infiltration twenty years or so ago, and she's been brought up from a baby by a Malaysian couple, the houseman and housekeeper of some friends of mine who've retired and gone back to England and have, so to speak, bequeathed her immediate future to me. As for her using the cottage, like our other Asian guests I think she'll prefer it, and I didn't suppose that our making a permanent threesome about the house and at meals would appeal to you.'

'No,' Sara agreed, wishing she could feel more welcome for the scheme on the face of it. 'What's her name?' she asked. 'And does she speak English?'

'Of course, I'm not wishing a savage on you. And her name—Kluai Mai. Mai for short.'

Sara made an effort. 'Mai—rather nice,' she said. 'And how well do you know her? When did you last see her?'

'Only once in the last six months, when the Bartrams, my friends, were leaving Malaya and the need for her advanced dance training came up. Anyway, Lim must meet her at the airport, and I'd like you to go along too. You'd probably like to have her to dinner on her first night, I daresay?'

'Of course. She'll feel strange.'

It was not until she was on her way to the airport with Lim the next evening that Sara admitted to herself that she hadn't asked Rede for a physical picture of the girl, *because she hadn't wanted to hear it.* While they had been talking a flash of memory had recalled his cryptic 'The Malaysian women are very beautiful. Seductive too——' and she had known that just then she couldn't bear to hear his not-so-long-ago impression of the eighteen-year-old Mai, Malaysian and a dancer. Nor had he volunteered one. Why not? She was afraid of knowing that too.

But evidently Lim was armed with the girl's description, for when the passengers from the plane came through to the visitors' barrier he bowed at once to a slight figure in a blue sari walking alone beside her porter. He brought her to Sara, standing a little apart from the crowd. Sara caught her breath, for Kluai Mai was indeed beauty in miniature—as delicately fashioned and coloured as a piece of fine porcelain; tiny, almost weighted down by a wealth of piled black hair, but hands and feet and features in perfect small-scale proportion. A child in stature, but a woman in figure—a woman whose looks Rede would have had to praise, if he had mentioned them at all ...

Sara offered her hand with a smile. 'I'm Sara, Rede Forrest's wife,' she said. 'And you are Kluai Mai?'

The girl smiled. 'Yes. But they call me Mai.'

'So Rede said. And I'd like to, if I may?'

'Please—I did not know that Mr Rede was married. He has not told us so.'

'I think,' said Sara, 'that when he saw you last, we weren't married. We met and were married in England only a month or two ago.'

Mai agreed, 'Yes, it was before that when he came to Kota Tingii and brought me to Singapore for my interview at the School.' Her eyes sparkled. 'You know that I was accepted and that I am to attend there on a course before I am professional and can make the dance my career?'

'Yes. Tell me about it, won't you, and what you'll be doing there?' Sara urged, glad to find a subject of conversation to occupy them on the return drive.

Mai was childishly and gratifyingly delighted with the cottage. 'For me! All my own!' her soft voice crooned. 'A door,' opening and shutting it several times—'and a lock and a key, and a couch and cushions and—what is that?' she asked, pointing.

'That' was a white-wrapped sheaf of flowers on a table. Sara took up the card which lay with it and passed it to the girl. Mai read aloud, 'To Mai from Rede. Happy landings for my orchid girl,' and snatched the paper from a single spray of orchids, deeply purple and white-hearted. Sara thought, He sent me flowers, but without a message—as Mai exulted, '*Dear* Mr Rede! They are for my name, you see. Kluai Mai means in English "orchid blossom". What does *your* name mean?' she asked Sara.

'I don't know. Do names have to mean something?'

Seriously, 'Always, in Malay and in Thai,' Mai assured her. 'We are named for flowers or jewels or birds. And I have a book, telling the meanings of names from all over the world. I must look for yours and shall tell you.'

'In the meanwhile, call me by it, won't you? And I'm sure Rede will want you to call him Rede, not "Mr" all the time,' said Sara.

'That will be for him to say,' Mai replied demurely.

After telling her they expected her to dinner and leaving her to more discovery of her domain, Sara reflected that it was impossible not to warm to her eager youth. At eighteen, if that were her age, she was not much Sara's junior, but seemingly without any of the problems Sara had already gathered to herself. She realised she had even made a troubling prejudice out of Rede's failure to describe Mai as the lovely that she was, and she had been ready to be hurt by his calling Mai his 'orchid girl'.

But what had she to fear? However slightly he knew the Mai of eighteen, he probably saw her as a child still and had known how she would appreciate his thought in making her welcome with her namesake flower. Rede had such urbane gestures at his fingertips, Sara knew, and it wasn't likely he would have rapturised over the looks of a mere child. There was nothing sinister to be questioned, after all. Nothing her jealousy needed to watch ...

When Mai came over to the house she had changed into a simple Western dress of soft crêpe, had let down her hair and tied it back with a wide ribbon bow, the effect being as young-teenage as was her plunge at Rede when they met, her arms flung round his neck, a kiss for each of his cheeks. He unclasped her hands and held her off from him. 'Such unbridled enthusiasm! What on earth have I done to deserve it?' he chided.

'Oh—my dear little house, Mr Rede——!'

'Rede and Sara——'

'Rede, then—And sending me orchids, and all your kindness to me, and Mrs—I mean Sara's too!'

He pinched her cheek and let her go. 'Well, cool it, lass,' he said paternally, 'and don't go overboard with thanks for what's going to be a hard grind while you're at it. For you're not going to turn out just "a" classical dancer. You're going to be "the" dancer of your year, and after that, the sky your limit. Understood?'

She blushed and dimpled. 'Understood,' she echoed, and Sara, reassured, thought, He sees her as someone to be educated, indulged a little, but disciplined. He's ambitious for her, as he might be for a talented child of his own. *If he and I ever have one*, the thought ended on a poignant awareness that on his side it wouldn't be a child of love.

Over dinner the talk was of Mai's plans and time-table. She would bicycle to the School every day to study posture and costume and mime as well as dancing, and would have the privacy of her cottage for practice and study.

'And I must find myself some pupils,' she claimed seriously at one point.

'Pupils?' echoed Rede. 'You're to be one yourself.'

'Ah, but I must earn some money. The expense of the School——'

'Forget the expense. That's been taken care of.'

'But to accept charity does not please me, and I must live. No,' Mai insisted firmly, 'I must pass on to some little children all I know. The School will be glad to find them for me, for they should all learn when they are very young. I myself began to be taught before I was five years old. Arm movements. Hands, fingers'—she demonstrated their suppleness—'we may not all become dancers, but all of us must learn. So please,' she appealed to Rede, 'I may take some children for lessons in my cottage?'

'Only if it doesn't interfere with your own work. Or proves too much for you.'

'It won't, I promise you. It will help me to practise,' she beamed, and turned to Sara.

'I looked in my book for your name. We haven't it in Malay, but in Arabic and Hebrew it means "princess". Does that please you?' she asked.

Sara laughed. 'I'm flattered!'

'You shouldn't be,' Mai assured her gravely. 'For you are like a princess—an English one, tall and fair and—and cool. Is she not?' she added to Rede.

'News to me that princesses are particularly cool.' Beneath half-lowered lids he affected to study Sara. 'But of Sara—yes, cool is a good description.'

'And you find her beautiful too? You married her for that?' Mai urged.

His eyes still upon Sara, 'And other reasons,' he said.

'But of course—there would be love as well,' Mai concluded happily as he stood and told her,

'Come along, it's time you were in bed. I'll see you home.'

Palms together beneath her chin, Mai bobbed Goodnight to Sara, who, while she waited for Rede's return, thought, 'Cool'? Would he have added 'calculating' if he had dared? Mai's naïve praise of her had meant 'poised', which Sara hoped she appeared, but Rede's echo and his look had had a different meaning that was all their own, and for only Sara to understand.

When he came back he poured drinks for them both. 'Well?' he said, and then, 'I suppose I should thank you for giving Mai a civilised reception— for resisting the urge to utter two faint cheers?'

'Why, what reception did you expect me to give her?' Sara queried.

He shrugged. 'On the principle that two women

are supposed to be unable to share a kitchen, they could find sharing a house even more unacceptable, couldn't they?'

'But you'd thought of that. Mai won't be sharing the house, you said?'

'An establishment, then. A domain. The area of sovereignty of one of them. You know very well what I mean.'

She did, Sara thought. He meant sharing his interest, his concern. Aloud she said, wanting his reaction, 'But Mai is hardly another woman. In some ways she seems very much a child.'

'At eighteen-plus—with those looks?'

Sara wished he had agreed with her about Mai's immaturity. 'Yes, why didn't you tell me what a beauty she is?' she asked.

'Probably because of the two women in a kitchen syndrome. You might have been prejudiced, without giving her a chance.'

'I see. The typical established cat's resentment of the intrusion of a kitten? Whereas in fact, you consider I've behaved quite nicely? Thank you. I'm—gratified.' She couldn't resist the irony.

He looked at her over the rim of his glass. 'Very nicely,' he agreed. 'According to Mai—like a princess. Noblesse oblige, and all that. You don't even question the "charity" that Mai resents so hotly. Beneath you to ask about it? More noblesse oblige, perhaps?'

Sara said, 'I didn't expect you to think it concerned me.'

'As my wife—no? In fact, since Mai's foster-parents couldn't possibly meet the cost, I'm sharing the expenses of her training with my friends, the Bartrams. And if there's any more chat from Mai about charity, I hope you won't listen. If she's half as good as I think she's going to be, she'll be no liability to our sponsorship of her. She'll be an investment——'

At the sound of the telephone Rede broke off and went to answer it. It was evidently a business call, a long one, and leaving him to it, Sara slipped from the room and went to bed.

How *did* he regard Mai? Her mind worried at the question before it allowed her to sleep. For all his apparent frankness he hadn't told her in so many words—that he saw the girl *only* as a naïve child, or *only* as a lovely young woman, or *only* as an asset to be nursed along to success. Something of all three, then? He had given no clue. He had complimented Sara on showing no jealousy—but how sincere had he been in that? Or had some sadistic urge to punish her *wanted* her to be jealous, with or without cause, and had been disappointed that she hadn't behaved like a shrew?

She didn't know, and he would not tell her. She felt newly empty of all knowledge of him, of his motives, his emotions, his needs. It was an emptiness which craved to be filled, but it was beyond her bewilderment of that night to foresee the how and the when of its filling.

Her last waking thought was that she would not,

could not, be jealous of Mai.

Later she was to question at what point she first
had cause to lose sight of that resolve. Had the
poison of suspicion begun working only with a certain enforced hour of Isabel Iden's company? Or
had she already become reluctantly watchful of
Mai's relationship with Rede—her obvious anxiety
to please him, her appealing dependence on his
praise? Or again, there had been a remark of George
Merlin's which had had no signficance for her at
the time—had her recollection of that sown a can-
ker in her mind, even before chance put it at the
mercy of Isabel's calculated hints?

The occasion was innocent enough. Ina Belmont,
in addition to her social activities, was a beaver of
industry in good works and charitable causes—one
of which was to be served by a bazaar in the garden
of her house. As usual she collected a posse of helpers
for the stalls, among them, this time, Sara as her
latest voluntary recruit.

Sara was to man a fancy-goods stall with another
young Temasik wife whom she liked. But on re-
porting for duty she found Isabel behind the display in the booth. 'Standing in for Connie West,
who's gone sick,' Isabel announced laconically.
'Pretty much of a bore, but Ina simply doesn't listen
when one says No. If you're ever tempted to try,
don't. It's only a waste of breath.'

The bazaar was duly opened by a Government
V.I.P.'s lady; the patrons circled and began to buy—

and then the rain, unkindly and unexpectedly so
early in the afternoon, began to fall. The patrons
drifted away; as many as Ina was able to collect
were herded into the marquee for a premature tea,
and Ina made a round of the stallholders, urging
courage and patience—a general instilling heart into his troops.

'It can't last long, and at least you're under cover
yourselves. At the first gleam of sun, they'll come
back, and at least the ones I've managed to capture
I'll *send* back, full of bonhomie and tea,' she promised as she sailed back to the marquee under the
shelter of a carriage umbrella.

Isabel sat back, offered cigarettes and lighted one.
'So much for a wasted afternoon. What could you
have done with it?' she asked Sara.

'Considering the rain, nothing much probably,'
replied Sara, forced to be civil, but wondering
whether Isabel remembered the scarcely veiled hostility of their last encounter, and whether she still
believed in Cliff's feet of clay.

But Isabel had a different line of attack today.
She said, 'The rain wouldn't matter, if you had
anyone exciting to take you out. But one hears
Rede is working all the hours there are, so when
you're bored, I suppose you can't look to him?'

'During the day, no,' said Sara. 'And I shouldn't
think of asking him.'

'Funny,' mused Isabel. 'When I used to come out
here before I married Cliff, I had only to lift the
phone and call Rede, and he would come running.

Times must have changed.'

'They have,' Sara agreed levelly. 'He says he's busier now and with more responsibility than for years past.'

'Or could that be a front that's been forced on him? I mean—a kind of escape route from *two* women at home in competition for his attention?'

'Two women?'

Isabel's eyes widened in question. 'Well, aren't there now? I mean, Rede may think he's made a master move, but it's asking rather a lot to expect people to swallow that the little Malay is merely a student he's sponsoring? Not to mention expecting too much of you, to harbour her under your own roof! What do they call that kind of threesome in French? *Une ménage à trois*, isn't that it? So difficult for you to explain away—Rede should know better. And really, you know, everyone will be agog to know how you let him sell you the idea. Or why, for that matter, he needed to, so soon after your whirlwind romance and your special licence marriage?'

Sara had felt her blood chill. 'It wasn't a special licence marriage,' she said. 'And what idea are you talking about?'

'Tch! You can't be that dumb!' Isabel scoffed.

'I don't think I am,' Sara said as evenly as she could. 'I know you're hinting at something pretty odious about Rede and myself and Kluai Mai, but you certainly owe me some plainer speaking than hints.'

'And be threatened with slander?' Isabel shook her head. 'Oh no, you don't get me that way, when you must know perfectly well what I mean about Rede's getting his cake and eating it. And though of course it's being done all over—which is why Temasik wants its staff to be married—it took Rede to think up the novelty of installing his young friend in his own house and asking his wife to chaperone her. Brilliant, that. Totally above suspicion! And when other men are making do with back-street, hole-and-corner afternoons, Rede is sitting pretty, rectitude personified, while you, my dear, mutt that you are, actually stand for it!'

'Stand for my husband's keeping his mistress in the same house as he keeps me—is that what you're saying?' Sara enquired.

Isabel shrugged. 'You said it. I didn't.'

'But it's what you meant. And how, in those circumstances, do you suggest they could meet there in secret without my knowing?'

'Oh dear, haven't the child's bijou quarters got a separate entrance? With a lock and key? Too remiss of Rede to have overlooked a detail like that.' Isabel's tone affected deep concern, rousing Sara to furious retort.

'They have—both a lock and a key,' she said tautly. 'When Kluai Mai isn't at school, she's usually in them; when Rede is at home we're mostly together, and when he isn't, it's seldom that I don't know where he is. But if there are any facts you still need to fill out your hints, why don't you ask

Rede for them to his face? I'll arrange for him to see you any time you wish.'

'As if he'd tell me, or admit anything! Be your age, do,' Isabel urged, adding, 'What's more, I'll take a bet *you* won't face Rede with any of this either. You'd be afraid to—either of his refusing to answer, or even more afraid of his admitting I'm right.'

'Which isn't remotely likely,' Sara claimed proudly.

'No? Though I rather wonder—You know, I do wonder whether, after chasing me without result for so long, he may have married you, not only on the rebound from me, but because he already had this set-up in view—import a wife first, and then, however attractive the young protegée may be, with everything above board and in the open, who's going to dare to throw any stones?'

'It doesn't seem to have deterred you,' Sara pointed out.

'I don't scandalmonger for the sake of it,' Isabel declared loftily. 'I've only tried to open your eyes in private to signposts which I'd have thought you could read for yourself. For instance, the Culture School doesn't train people for fun. So how is the girl being financed? Never asked yourself that? Nor asked Rede?'

'Rede and his friends the Bartrams are sharing the cost.'

'Phooey! I've met them, and they're quite old. Only missionaries, at that. But if that's what Rede has told you, believe him, do. It's you who have to live with him, after all.' Isabel stubbed her cigarette, stretched and went to the front of the stall. 'It's stopped raining,' she announced. 'Now Ina had better produce some customers, or I'm packing it in and going home.' She had filled an idle hour to her evident satisfaction. The same hour for Sara had crystallised doubts and fears which she wouldn't have admitted to Isabel for the world.

But now they were there in her mind, poisoned darts at the ready. There was George Merlin's boast of his freedom to keep a mistress on the premises, whereas men in the city needed the respectable cover of a wife for their affairs. There was Mai's freedom to come and go and to entertain whom she pleased in the cottage. There were hours of Sara's own absence from the house when Rede could visit her there. They could even meet in the city when Mai was supposed to be at school. There was Mai's uninhibited admiration of Rede, and even her assumption of his and Sara's ideally happy marriage could be a front of flattery for Sara's deception. There was Rede's lie—if it were a lie—that the responsibility for Mai's expenses was not his alone. (And if it weren't a lie, why had he pressed Sara to ask the question, if not to satisfy himself that she believed what he wanted her to?)

And—worst of all—Isabel's shrewd guess at Rede's purpose in marrying her was confirmed by a truth which she knew. Before he had met her or proposed to her, he had arranged for Mai to come to Singapore; had allotted her the cottage, and so found himself with a 'use' for a wife which would stifle gossip at its source. Against all Sara's fairer judgment of both Rede and Mai, it all seemed to add up.

In this new light, unable to resist a temptation to watch them together, on arriving home she pushed a note under Mai's door, asking her to dinner. Rede was not yet in when the girl came over to the house, so was not there to hear her bubble, 'This is my lucky day—the evening with you both tonight, and lunch with Rede this morning! He had to go down to the docks on business, so he called in at the School and took me out.'

Would Rede have told her this? Sara wondered. Yet how could she suspect Mai's eager blurting of it? 'Where did you go?' she asked.

'Into Chinatown. We had laksa. You know laksa?'

Sara thought she did. 'Isn't it noodles with spiced coconut sauce and herbs?' she suggested.

'Yes—a Nonya dish. That's Chinese food, cooked Malay style. You should taste *my* laksa—I make it deliciously. Don't I?' Mai appealed to Rede, who came in just then.

Sara held her breath for his reply but learned nothing from it. 'Do you?' he said carelessly.

Mai's pretty lips formed a childish pout. 'You have forgotten that when you came to Kota Tingii in January I cooked a meal for you and you said then that it was—"out of this world"? A funny saying, I thought. But it means very good, perfect, does it not?'

Sara breathed more freely. So—no clandestine meals *à deux* when she herself was not around. Nothing for suspicion there. Nor was there throughout Mai's evening with them. She chattered dance techniques to Rede and clothes and food talk to Sara. She invited Sara to what would amount to her passing-out parade at the end of the month, a dance display after which she would end her novice status, could take on some pupils and might be chosen for some occasional paid engagements. When she left Rede went with her, and Sara bade him goodnight, saying she was going to bed.

But in her room moonlight was striking silver bars across bed and floor, and without switching on the light, she went over to the balcony and out into the warmth of the night. She leaned on the little balustrade, watching for Rede's return from the cottage. It stood at right angles to the main building and in the moonlight the doorway was fully visible. But there was no movement there; the door was closed; the cottage was lighted and Sara calculated that it was impossible for Rede to have regained the house in the few minutes it had taken her to come upstairs. That meant——? All her sick doubts returned.

She blamed herself. She had told Mai she was going to bed, and so wouldn't know how long Rede stayed. He was still there: that was certain now. She stared at the door, willing it to open 'before

I've counted ten', she begged of Fate. But though the sheer concentration of her gaze tricked her more than once into believing it did open, she could have counted to ten many times before Rede's figure was silhouetted against the light behind him and he came out.

How much time had passed? Half an hour at least. Sara darted back into her bedroom, thankful she had not switched on there, as Rede would conclude she was already asleep and would go straight to his room. Very quietly she unzipped her long dress, but it must have made a whisper on the floor as she stepped out of it, for without knowing whether he had come upstairs or not, she could almost *feel* him pause at the door before he opened it and came in.

'Why in the dark?' He flicked a switch, revealing her standing in her slip, her dress over her arm. 'Not undressed yet? I thought I'd find you in bed.'

She mustn't admit the moonlight had tempted her on to the balcony, or he would guess she had spied on him. 'Yes, well, I didn't come up straight away,' she lied. 'And when I did, the moonlight was bright enough to undress by, and it seemed a pity to shut it out.'

'So it does.' His finger went to the switch again, returning the room to moonlight and shadow. Dear God, she almost prayed, let him want to tell me why he was so long with Mai! But as he crossed the floor to her it was clear he had no such intent in mind. In silence he unzipped the strapless bodice of her slip, kicked it aside and pressed her back towards the bed. She sank down upon it, and he leaned over her, his touch upon arms and breast and slender torso a tinder, as ever, for her senses.

He murmured thickly, 'Moonlight is wasted on anything as prosaic as undressing to no purpose,' and brought his lips to part hers in searching, arrogant demand of her response.

She thought of him, 'To come to me, straight from Mai!' And of herself, 'Hateful, hateful—to want him as I do!' She felt her body had betrayed her to him, but as always in his arms there was heightening sensual delight for her and her gift to him of surrender, and afterwards a peace that she could only hope he knew too.

CHAPTER FIVE

IN her half-sleep that night Sara was aware of a physical unease as well as the turmoil of her thoughts, and when she woke fully in the morning her arms, shoulders, neck and face were afire with irritation. She reached for her hand-mirror and gasped at what it showed. She was covered with angry blotches which looked like mosquito bites, and suddenly she recalled how one, or perhaps more than one had zoomed in the darkness round her as she had been out on the balcony. Yet in her agonised concentration of watching for Rede, she hadn't even noticed she had been stung.

She went to the bathroom cabinet for calomine, found the bottle empty and met Malee bringing in her morning tea as she came back.

Malee almost dropped her tray in her shocked dismay. 'Mem! Mem! Your face! You have fever! Get back into bed, mem, please. I tell Tuan Forrest and he will come,' she exclaimed.

'No, Malee, don't——' The shame of having Rede see her like this! But Malee was already knocking at his inner door, making staccato explanations, and the next minute Rede, dragging the sash of his robe about him, was at her bedside. Malee discreetly departed.

Rede touched Sara's cheek with gentle fingers. 'How did this happen? You can't have slept under your net,' he accused.

'I did. I must have been stung last night. I heard some mosquitoes about,' she confessed.

'Here in the room?'

'No. On the balcony.'

'But I thought you'd only just come upstairs when I found you undressing?'

Caught out in her lie! 'Yes, well, I did go out on the balcony before I began to undress.'

'And stayed there long enough to collect this lot even after hearing the things on the prowl?'

'I suppose so.' She paused. Then, since she had been found out, she put the ball into his court. 'I—saw you leave the cottage,' she said.

'Yes, I was there longer than I meant to be. Mai had had some bad news and wanted help and advice.'

If he was lying, he was doing it well. 'Bad news? What about? She seemed happy enough at dinner,' said Sara.

'About her foster-mother. When she got in from school she found your note on her mat, but missed a mailed letter from her foster-father. She found it when she went in last night. As you know, when the Bartrams went back to England, he took a job on a rubber estate where he and Suki Ying, his wife, have a bungalow on the plantation. But now she's gone down with fever, and I'm arranging to take Mai back to see her today. It's more than half a day's journey, so I'll stay overnight and we'll come back tomorrow.'

'Where will you stay?'

'There's a hotel of sorts in Kota Tingii.'

'And Mai?'

'She'll want to stay at the bungalow. Meanwhile, you're to stay in bed, and before I leave I'll call the doctor to you.'

'For a few insect bites? I've done my anti-malarial dope course,' Sara protested.

'Maybe. But Doc will give you an antibiotic jab in case you contacted a rogue mosquito that was immune to the dope, and he'll keep an eye on you for the next few days.' Rede pointed to the tray which Malee had left on the bedside table. 'Ring for some more tea if that's cold. I'll look in on you again before I go,' he said, and went back to his own room.

So he had had good reason for staying with Mai last night, Sara thought as she lay back in bed. While she had suspected him she had dreaded having to meet Mai on normal terms, but he had been so casual and open that she was glad she had forbidden herself the temptation of asking either him or Mai some shrewish questions. But how long would it take her to forget Isabel Iden's poison—if she ever did, while Rede gave her no positive sign of his needing her for more than her body and her use to him as a duenna for Mai?

Later Buppa came to ask what she would like for a light lunch and to cluck her commiseration at Sara's bloated appearance. A sheaf of delicate lotus blossom arrived with Rede's dry message on its accompanying card—'That will teach you to try conclusions with the local *culicidae* after dark'— typical of his surface attentiveness, that he should have found time to have the florist send it. And the doctor called, gave an injection, prescribed a lotion to be used at night, told Sara she could get up for an evening meal in a robe if she liked, and promised to call again the next day.

The effect of the injection was to make her sleepy and she drowsed through most of the afternoon and early evening until, when dusk had fallen, she pulled on a negligee and stepped into mules and went downstairs.

She dined from a tray and drowsed again in front

of the television set for she didn't know how long. It was still working without an audience when she came to with a start at Malee's gentle, 'Mem— please?'

She knuckled sleep from her eyes. 'Yes, Malee? What time is it?'

'Nearly nine o'clock, mem. But, mem——?'

'Yes?'

'In the hall there is someone to see you. He comes, he says, with a message from Tuan Forrest. I tell him you are not well, but he says he should see you. It is important that he does.'

Sara frowned. 'I can't see him—I'm not dressed. Who is he? Did you ask his name?'

'Yes, I remember it. He calls one time on the telephone. Tuan Iden,' nodded Malee.

Cliff? With a message for her from Rede! From Rede, who had been on the mainland since morning; and Cliff, the least likely person for him to employ on such an errand? Sara's reason rejected the idea outright, and she told Malee too sharply, 'I can't see Mr Iden. If he has a message, ask him to write it down, or tell you what it is, will you, please?'

Malee stood her ground. 'It is very important, he says, that he give it to yourself, mem——' she had begun when Cliff appeared at the door of the room and, since she couldn't brawl with him in front of Malee, Sara had no choice but to acknowledge him. She nodded to him; Malee effaced herself and Cliff came across the room.

Sara said, 'I don't think you can have a message for me from Rede. You haven't, have you?'

Cliff shook his head. 'It was the only reason for your seeing me which I hoped you would believe. I had to use it.'

'Why?'

'Because you wouldn't see me the last time I rang you and asked you. I'm sorry, Sara. Rede said what had happened to you when he came into the office before he left for the mainland. He's having to stay overnight, isn't he? So I saw this as my only chance to get to see you alone. That was why I lied to your maid,' Cliff said wretchedly.

Sara stood up, drew her robe about her and indicated her face. 'You can see the state I'm in. I'm due to go back to bed. But to see me alone, to say what?' she asked.

'Much the same as before, only more so.'

'You mean you haven't managed to convince Isabel that you aren't having an affair with me?'

'I think she wouldn't mind getting evidence that I am, but without it there's nothing she can do. That's why *she* mustn't know either that I've come to you tonight. But no, it's the other thing now—her conviction that it's your power behind Rede's throne that's keeping me down at Temasik. And "down" is the operative word. I'm not in his confidence; I never deputise for him. Today, for instance, he passed me over for another chap to take on his appointments. None of which I can justify to Isabel without her blaming you.'

Sara offered scant sympathy. 'Too bad,' she said. 'But the situation is still the same. If you are being "kept down" at Temasik, you must tell Isabel it's through no influence of mine.'

'And there's nothing you could do the other way, perhaps? For instance, put in a casual word as to when I'm going to get a bit of executive status, or something like that?' Cliff pleaded.

'It wouldn't do any good.' What a craven she had been saved from marrying! thought Sara.

'Even though Isabel is threatening to leave me, if I don't get a square deal from Rede soon? She's as serious as that!'

'Moral blackmail won't get you anywhere,' Sara told him coldly. 'Anyway, what about the George Merlin opening? If Isabel is dissatisfied with your chances at Temasik, why don't you take that up?'

'Because Merlin has only put out feelers so far; he hasn't made me a firm offer, and with Isabel's expensive tastes I can't afford to cut my losses at Temasik and risk being out of a job.' Head lowered, fists thrust into jacket pockets, Cliff paced to a near wall and back again. 'If only Isabel wouldn't *nag* so!' he muttered, and then intensely, 'Oh, *Sara!*' as he halted before her and his hands shot out to take her by the shoulders, drawing her into his arms.

'You're hurting me!' The pain for her burning skin was her first reaction, her second, her mental revulsion at his touch, did not register with him in time to check his continuing murmur of, 'The utter fool I was ever to let you go, Sara. To choose Isabel instead of keeping you—damned, damned fool!' before his lips took hers in a lingering kiss.

'Don't!' She wrenched her mouth free and struggled. But he was too strong for her and it was so, held fast as he kissed her straining throat, that to her horror she saw that Rede had come in and was watching them.

From just inside the door he uttered two words—to Cliff. 'Get—out,' he said, his pause between the words and their emphasis a threat which Cliff could not fail to understand. He released Sara, stood awkwardly for a moment or two, and then, offering neither defence to Rede nor apology to her, he slunk past Rede and went out.

He left Sara panting with anger. How dared he crawl away like a whipped puppy at Rede's say-so? She couldn't wait to explain to Rede, but Cliff's leaving her to do it alone was as despicable as his hysterical forcing of her. It was all of a piece with his ruse of getting to see her alone and it put him beneath her contempt. Rede must see that ...

But Rede, crossing the room to stand over her, made it clear that, whatever he thought of Cliff, he had already judged her on what he had seen.

'Sit down,' he ordered her. She sat down. 'I thought you would have been told to stay in bed today?'

'I was, but the doctor said I could get up this evening if I cared to.'

'And you "cared to" as soon as you saw yourself with the rare chance to entertain your late lover while I was away?'

'I——'

His glance appraised her negligee, the low-cut nightgown beneath it. 'Charming déshabille,' his sarcasm approved. 'Though if you hadn't meant to dress with any more formality than that, I wonder you didn't invite him to your bedroom instead.'

Aghast, 'I didn't invite him! Nor plan to entertain him,' she denied, making every word count, she hoped. 'He came uninvited and tricked Malee into letting him in, saying he had to see me—and alone.'

'Knowing, as of course you both did, that I expected to be away for the night. Too harsh luck for you, wasn't it, that Mai decided she wanted to stay with her people for a few days, leaving me free to come back? And even if you didn't invite him, he seems to have chanced his arm to some purpose, to judge by the tableau I happened upon——'

That infuriated her. 'You think I let him make love to me? That I encouraged him? And—well, look at me as I am tonight,' she demanded, underlining her meaning by throwing open her robe, offering her neck and shoulders for his inspection— 'In this state, do you suppose I'd expose myself to or welcome any man's lovemaking—*any* man's at all?'

Rede allowed coolly, 'Feminine vanity being what it is, you have a point. But if opportunities are hard to come by and the need is urgent, I'd have thought a mere rash of insect bites wouldn't prove much of a deterrent.'

'Then you *don't* believe me?' she flared.

'Difficult to credit that you weren't flattered by the man's revived interest in you. Not his first attempt at contact, was it? And there have been others more successful since, perhaps?'

Sara's head went up proudly. 'None for the purpose of his making love to me. Nor was there tonight,' she said.

'So you'd have me believe the passionate clinch was only a by-product of some other tense situation between you? What was it?'

But Sara had remembered the word she had given to Cliff on Sentosa that his confidences were safe with her, and even to justify herself with Rede, she would not go back on it. Besides, Rede had no right to doubt her when she spoke the truth. She had been angry and contemptuous of Cliff, but Rede's refusal to believe her humiliated her beyond measure. If he wanted to know what errand had brought Cliff to her, let him ask Cliff about it or go without knowing. He was not going to hear it from her!

'I can't tell you that,' she said. 'It's Cliff's own business, not mine.'

'I see. Business for tête-à-tête discussion at night, and to be sealed with a tender embrace for another man's wife, for whom he had little enough use a while back?' Rede shrugged. 'Well, you're entitled to your vow of silence, of course, though it doesn't do much for your case, would you say?'

'For my *case*?' she echoed indignantly.

'Of innocent non-complicity in anything but tea and sympathy for friend Iden's problems——'

Proof that he hadn't believed a word she had said in her defence! Utterly outraged, Sara demanded, 'And when—*when*, as your wife, do I have to make a "case" for myself when I'm telling the truth? Or' —bitterly, as a thought struck her—'would you prefer that I should be lying, and that I want to take Cliff back as my lover, because that would free you of the obligations you undertook when you married me?'

'And do you suppose that, wanting to be free of them, I'd have to make your infidelity my excuse, if or when?' he parried.

'You could probably convince yourself it was your reason, not your excuse!'

'Neither of which I'm pleading at the moment— being reasonably content with my bargain so far.'

'Thank you.' She waited, praying the impossible —that he would enlarge on that; tell her he accepted that she hadn't lied; say something which would bridge the gulf between them. But when he was silent, she had to continue to worry at an argument which dignity should have left where it was.

'And if that's meant to exonerate me, I suppose you mean to take the rest of the "case" out on Cliff?' she queried.

'As I see fit,' Rede nodded.

'And how will that be?'

'It'll ensure that if he gatecrashed tonight and misunderstood the warmth of your welcome, it won't happen again. Also he'll understand that any private business between you and him must be my affair too—and mine first.'

'And you think he'll agree to that?'

'Why not? Placed as he is in relation to my wife and to me and to the firm, he can hardly fail to agree, I imagine,' Rede replied almost blandly, as if his meaning hadn't a menace all its own. Then, crossing to the main light-switch and with a finger on it, he continued, 'And now it's time you were back where you'll be exposed to no man's unwelcome attentions—your room and your bed,' and he held out his other hand to her.

She went to him and took it, almost drowning in the flood of contradictory emotion he aroused in her—resentment, love, challenge, passion—and longing for the giving of his hand to mean more than it did, his fingers the merest light touch upon hers in a clasp which was only guiding her up the stairs.

A few days later she received a stiffly-worded letter of apology from Cliff for his 'uncalled-for intrusion' upon her. She had no doubt that its sending had been a forfeit exacted by Rede, showing that his grilling of Cliff had convinced him of the truth of her version. But she destroyed the letter and did not mention it to Rede. Nor did he to her. Evidently he had dealt with the incident to his satisfaction and did not feel he owed her an apology of his own for having doubted her word. Or had the sheaf of dark red roses with no message which he had sent her the next day been meant as his *mea culpa*? She had thanked him for them but had scorned to ask. Either scorned, or dreaded a reply which would not tell her anything she desperately wanted to hear. He allowed flowers to speak for him too often, and without love as their language, their beauty was no more than a mockery.

It was a week before Rede went back to the mainland to fetch Mai, and during that time Sara made a conscious effort to rid her thoughts of the churning poison which Isabel had stirred up.

Of course it was only natural for Rede to have spent time with Mai after the shock of the girl's hearing about her foster-mother's illness. And if he hadn't had good reason, would he have been indiscreet enough to stay so long at that time of night, with Sara herself perhaps awaiting his return, even though she had gone up to bed? Another thought—would he dare to judge her so harshly if he were guilty of infidelity himself? And though she wasn't too sure of that last reasoning—men had double standards in such matters, she knew—it all helped her to welcome Mai's return warmly and sincerely.

It was ironic that it should be kindly Ina Belmont, not Isabel, who was to add fresh fuel to the embers of her jealousy of Mai.

Since Mai's first arrival, Ina had been interested

in her and had invited her out to meet other young people at picnics and at her house. And it was after one such date for Mai that Ina commented worriedly to Sara,

'That child is unhappy. She's lost a lot of spirit since she went back to Kota Tongii. Have you any idea as to the cause?'

Sara hadn't noticed a change in Mai and said so. At which Ina conjectured, 'Could be it's nothing to do with her trip to the mainland, but simply a worsening case of hopeless hero-worship. Or hadn't you noticed either that she's suffering from that?'

'Hero-worship?' Sara questioned. 'Of whom?'

'Of Rede, of course,' Ina returned bluntly. 'For her, the sun rises and sets at his approval of her. It's a common teenage complaint, very painful at the time. Didn't you ever suffer from it? I had it badly for my music tutor at school, and did it hurt when he didn't even notice the sheep's eyes I made at him until I got over it, as one grows out of growing pains!'

Sara managed a faint smile to cover her dismay. 'Supposing he had noticed you and—well—encouraged you, would you have flattered yourself he was in love with you? Or might he even have been? In love with you, I mean?'

Ina shook a vigorous head. 'No chance of that, and I don't know that I ever wanted more than to shine and to succeed for him. As Mai does for Rede, and is dispirited for the same cause—that she recognises that in his eyes you'll always outshine her in everything. No, he loves you, and she knows it. Accepts it too, and isn't even jealous of you in the ordinary sense; only competing for the bit of him that she needs to admire and praise her work.'

'Where I'm in no competition with her at all,' mused Sara, taking heart if Ina's theory were true.

'Exactly,' Ina agreed. 'Knowing Rede for the perfectionist he is, she wants to be perfect too. All very natural at her age, but in a very little while she ought to be taking up with a boy-friend. We must find one for her. I'll look into it,' Ina concluded.

All of which Sara might have allowed to be reassuring if it hadn't proved to her that other people were aware of the closeness between Mai and Rede. Which meant that it showed, exposing her to the malice of Isabel and the idle speculations, if no worse, of their friends. But even then she might have discounted it and taken comfort in Ina's perceptive judgment if chance had not shattered the faith in Rede's loyalty which she was struggling to gain and keep.

Mai was to join them for dinner one evening when Sara had been to an afternoon concert with Ina. After it she had gone back to Ina's house for tea; some friends of Ina's had dropped in for drinks, and Sara reached home only shortly before Buppa would expect to serve the meal.

Sara hurried to the kitchen. 'Hold things back a little, please,' she told Buppa. 'Is Tuan Forrest in yet?'

Buppa turned down heat and adjusted the position of the pots and pans on her cooker. 'Tuan home, yes,' she said. 'Missee Mai come too. They in the garden, but they come in now, I think. Mem tell when she is ready for me to serve—yes?'

'Very shortly,' Sara promised. 'I must freshen up a bit first.' But before she went upstairs she went to the west-facing room where she and Rede usually met for a drink before dinner.

The sun, a fiery ball almost at horizon level, was casting long deep shadows across the room, causing Sara to halt at the door and adjust her vision to the semi-darkness within.

As she expected, Rede and Mai were there, two figures in silhouette, not sitting apart from each other with glasses in their hands, but standing close; no distance between their bodies, Mai's tiny head and face lowered and hidden by Rede's embracing arms, Mai's lime-juice and Rede's Daiquiri discarded on a low table beside them.

Sara, ready to greet Mai, caught the breath which would have sounded the words. She stood transfixed; they hadn't heard her at the door; they weren't facing her way. Now Rede was smoothing the ebony sheen of Mai's hair; she nestled her hidden face still closer to his chest, and Sara, her heart pounding in hammer strokes against her ribs, turned and fled.

So it was true! Isabel knew it. Ina Belmont too, and how many others? Isabel had minced no words about it; Ina must have tried to warn her with understatements about its being only a one-sided hero-worship on Mai's part, while knowing all the while of Rede's involvement in it. So how many others of their friends were sniggering behind their hands at Rede's adroit coup in putting Mai under his own roof without having to stoop to calling her his 'cook'—when 'protegée' was so much more acceptable a term!

Sara went about her brief toilet with mechanical haste, her thoughts almost a physical weight of pain inside her. She had to face the other two across her own dining-table, be pleasant with Mai, make conversation with Rede; take food and drink which, provided by him, ought to choke her, and watch ... watch every glance or gesture they exchanged.

On her way downstairs again it struck her that if Rede loved her, at sight of her and Cliff together, he could have suffered as she was doing now. But he did not love her. He had never claimed he did. Only that he had bought rights in her and was satisfied with his deal.

She went straight to the dining-room, asking Buppa to serve the first course after she had called Rede and Mai to the table. But neither of them appeared until after the food was brought, and then it was Rede who arrived alone, having taken an inordinately long time to cross the hall.

Sara's lifted brows asked the question which he answered as he sat down. 'Mai did turn up, but I've taken her home again,' he said. 'As you weren't in, we had a drink together, but she must have been overworking, catching up after her time out on the mainland. She was weepy and nervy and at last said she couldn't face eating with us tonight, and asked you to excuse her, if you would.' He helped himself to the chicken rice handed by Buppa, and began to eat.

'Is she ill?' Sara asked too sharply.

'I don't think so.'

(Nor do I, was Sara's caustic but unspoken thought.) Aloud she said, 'Because if she is, you shouldn't have let her go back to the cottage to be alone. I'd better go to her.'

There was a pause. 'I shouldn't, if I were you,' Rede said.

'Why not? Are you afraid I might question her as to why she was in your arms in the garden-room just now?'

Rede looked up from his plate. 'You saw us?' he asked.

'You didn't hear me. I came to the door.'

'And misread what you saw?'

Sara held his gaze with her own, hoping she could force him to remember the scene with Cliff. 'An unexpected onlooker sometimes does, some-times not,' she said.

'And on this occasion *did*,' he said.

'Then you weren't——? Mai wasn't——?'

'——Was merely needing a shoulder to cry on,' he cut into her pause. 'Yours, anyone's, would have done as well in the welter of self-pity and self-blame she's indulging at the moment.'

Could Sara believe him? Had he really been

caught by ill chance, as she had been with Cliff, or
was he making a clever case for himself and Mai?
And if Mai had only needed sympathy, what had
shamed her into refusing to spend the evening with
them?

Sara asked Rede that and he said, 'In fact, I
sent her home. If she had stayed, you would only
have condoled with her, and it's bracing, not sympathy, she needs. "Needs" as opposed to "wants",
that is.'

'*You* were condoling with her,' Sara reminded
him.

'In the stress of the moment, affording her a few
pats on the head and the usual "There, theres" in
the face of trouble.' (How plausible was that? Or
how true? Sara wondered.) He went on, 'But that
did nothing at all for her mood, and being, in her
right mind, a sensible girl, she knows she has to
work through this lot for herself.'

(If he were guilty, could he sound so prosaic, so
hard?) 'Through which lot?' Sara questioned, her
doubts of him on the wane.

'This conviction she's nursing, that she's no good
as a dancer; that she'll never make any sort of
grade, least of all the top one. She's even talking
of giving up the School and going home—which
would be madness.'

That could be true, if there were a liaison between them, and Mai felt guilty about it, thought
Sara, her doubts veering again. 'And would you
consent to that?' she asked Rede.

'Of course not,' he snapped. 'She's a natural, and it would be criminal to encourage her to abandon her career at this stage. I've attended some of her rehearsals at the School, and there's no doubt she has what it takes. No, she's staying here, as I've told her.'

It was news to Sara that he had kept in such close touch with Mai's progress. Neither of them had mentioned it ... In an effort to probe the truth even further, she asked, 'Have you ever thought that Mai could be lonely in the cottage? That she might be happier with the other trainees of her year in the Dance School's hostel?'

As if he sensed that his answer was important, Rede took time to consider the question before he parried it with one of his own. 'Does that mean *you* wouldn't mind being rid of her?' he queried.

Startled, Sara blushed. 'I? Why no,' she denied. 'Why should I want her to go? I'm—very fond of her. It's just that there must be some reason for her losing all that bubbling enthusiasm she came with, and it occurred to me that loneliness could be it. An idea, that's all,' she finished lamely.

Rede shook his head. 'She's not lonely, and while she is wallowing in this slough, I'm keeping an eye on her. She'll pull out of it; she knows she can dance, that it's the best thing she does, and I'll back her not to let any of us down when the crunch comes.' He paused. 'This passing-out concert, for instance. That's a kind of watershed for her. Once successfully on the other side of it, she'll be all right, particularly if we're both there, rooting for her for all we're worth. You've got it as a date? You won't miss it on any account?'

'Of course not,' Sara assured him, still no nearer to knowing whether he was dispassionately concerned for Mai, or whether he was papering over the facts of their affair.

His tone of voice had ordered her, rather than advised her, not to attempt to see Mai. But after they had both gone to their rooms that night, Sara knew she was not going to be able to sleep until she had seen the girl, whatever the outcome. Mai, guiltily unhappy for love of Rede, or Mai, unhappy for loss of faith in herself, must surely prove more vulnerable to questioning than Rede had been. Which meant that when she met him tomorrow Sara would be on the firm ground of knowing the truth—either way, and she could not wait.

There was no sound from Rede's room as she slipped quietly from her own. Behind the curtains of the cottage a light still burned, but there was no answer to Sara's soft knock upon the door. She knocked again without result, then tried the handle which, to her surprise, turned. The key which had so delighted Mai when she took over the place had not been used tonight. Had Mai been expecting a clandestine visitor—Rede? But when Sara stepped into the living-room on to which the door gave it was clear that Mai had not sat up waiting for anyone, for through the half-open door to the bedroom Sara could see her prone and asleep fully dressed, her face turned sideways upon her crossed arms.

Sara tiptoed nearer without her waking. The flesh above her delicate cheekbones was puffed and tears still glistened on her lashes. Without locking her door or switching off her light or undressing, she must have dropped asleep in the exhaustion of some despair which Sara couldn't bring herself to probe by waking her and asking the questions she had intended.

She went back into the living-room, hesitant and wishing she had not come. A now familiar aroma hung upon the air—the scent of the sticks of perfumed wood which the custom of Mai's religion burned in supplication to its Buddha. Mai must have been praying for help ... She had also, it seemed, used a joss-stick as a taper to burn a pile of paper scraps in the waste-backet, Sara noticed. On the table was an unburned sheet with a line or two of Mai's fine disjointed script upon it——

'Please, dear Rede, let me go,' Sara read. 'I am no good to you. There is no future for——'

That was all. Mai had abandoned it there. Sara re-read the words over and over, asking herself whether or not they answered the questions she had come to ask Mai—was Rede in love with her? Did she love him?

Sara left the cottage, still not knowing but fearing.

CHAPTER SIX

THERE was little doubt, Sara felt, that the papers Mai had burned had been her earlier attempts to write to Rede. Would they have been more explicit as to their relationship than the one the girl had abandoned on the table? Sara wondered, until her judgment of it was utterly bemused.

It was like a misspelt word, stared at for too long, which seemed to defy correction. 'Dear Rede'—that meant nothing sinister in Mai's openly affectionate phraseology; Sara had often heard her address Rede so. 'Let me go'. Rede himself admitted that she wanted to quit the School, but it could mean she was struggling in vain, against her own will and his, to part from him. 'I am no good to you.' 'Good' to his ambitious concern for her? Or 'good' to his need *of* her? And 'There is no future for——' That broken sentence could have ended in the clarity which Sara sought. But Mai had not finished it, leaving Sara's doubts where they were, and somehow by morning, after a night when the few words had turned to a meaningless jumble in her dreams, she had lost the spirit to pursue the search to certainty.

She would wait for more evidence that her fears were real, and if that were rank cowardice, so it had to be. She had become a coward. The dread of losing Rede to another woman had made her one.

In the days which followed neither his nor Mai's outward manner betrayed anything. Whatever her private troubles, in Sara's presence Mai hid them behind a serene, readily smiling face. She went to dance school every day as usual and claimed in Sara's hearing that she was practising hard. Rede seemed satisfied that his dealing with her misgivings was having effect, and he did not discuss them with Sara again.

He brought none of his business affairs home with him either, so that it was from Isabel, met by chance in a department store, that Sara heard first that Cliff was leaving Temasik.

'Well, apart from passing over Cliff whenever he could, for about a month now Rede has made his position intolerable,' Isabel complained. 'Round about then Rede had him on the carpet—Cliff said it was a private clash between them and wouldn't tell me what—and ever since he's been able to do nothing right. And when George Merlin at last came across with an offer to him, I made Cliff tell Rede he wanted out and Rede has let him go. I'd have thought Rede would tell you. Hasn't he?'

Sara began, 'I've told you before—he doesn't discuss his work or the personnel with me——'

'Huh! Cliff—mere "personnel" trash to you now? Dearie me, just how detached can we get, once we've married the boss!' scoffed Isabel as Sara controlled herself enough to continue,

'What will Cliff be doing for George Merlin?'

'As if you're interested! Cliff *will* be flattered! Anyway, he'll be superintending the freightage of orchids for shipment abroad and he'll be accompanying some of the consignments. Fabulous pay too, *and* a smack in the eye for Temasik, losing a man who might have been one of their brighter boys to Merlin Enterprises,' Isabel claimed.

'But they're not in competition. Temasik doesn't deal in orchid export,' Sara pointed out.

'Though how they'd like to, if Merlin hadn't cornered the market. Just watch Rede's reaction when he hears Cliff is going over to the enemy. Me, I can hardly wait!' triumphed Isabel before going on her way.

In fact, had she been present, she might have been surprised by Rede's 'reaction' to Sara's mention of the news, which he claimed to know already.

'It's a pity that if Iden wanted to get into orchids, he didn't wait until we went into exporting them ourselves,' he commented calmly.

'I thought Isabel said George Merlin had all the trade there was?' Sara queried.

'Pretty well all the local and mainland output— yes, I daresay,' Rede agreed. 'But Temasik is in process of drawing up contracts with a big group of Thailand growers, and if they go through, we shall be in a totally new export market, with the sky the limit. Iden should have bided his time a bit longer.'

'But he couldn't have known about this?'

'Of course not. It's still at hush-hush boardroom

level. Anyhow, he was always something of a square peg in his job. I thought when I trained him he had the makings of a good man, but he's only mediocre, and Isabel has too many delusions of grandeur to be the right wife for a mere junior who isn't going to make the grade.'

That was a chance to ask him about Isabel. 'You know her—or did know her—well enough to be able to say that?' Sara ventured.

'I think so. I saw a good deal of her—or rather she saw to it that I did—when she came out to her relatives every year. Wherever I looked, there the girl was, as russet-and-cream and willowy as a woman in a Burne-Jones painting, and just about as cold.'

That bore out Ina Belmont's version of their relationship and contradicted Isabel's own. Carefully, her spirit lifting a little, Sara asked, 'You weren't ever attracted to her yourself?'

'Attracted to—no. Interested in—yes, as a type.'

'Which was?'

'What she is now—still sexlessly lovely, ambition-ridden and as restless as a moth lacking a candle to flutter at.'

'Oh——' Taken slightly aback by so crisp a measurement of Isabel, Sara said, 'That sounds as cut-and-dried as if you were in the habit of type-casting people by private computer. Did you slot me into it somewhere when we met?'

His long look studied her. Then, 'No', he said. 'That day my computer went on the blink.'

'But since?' For almost the first time they were

on the verge of badinage and, high upon the relief that he hadn't ever cared for Isabel, Sara felt bold.

'Since then,' he said, 'its assessment has varied. But I'd have thought the general trend was plain enough?'

Her brief euphoria faded. 'Yes. Yes, it has been—quite plain,' she admitted.

'You'd rather I didn't spell it out in clear?'

Expect him to enlarge upon the contempt in which he held her? Never! 'No, thank you. I think I know—have known for some time what you think of me and where I stand with you,' she said.

It was a lie. But pride had dictated it.

On the day of Mai's passing-out concert, which she had ringed in her diary as a date not to be missed, there was nothing to warn Sara that the ill fate which dogged her brittle relationship with Rede was to be at work again.

Mai, whatever her inner turmoil, seemed to be suffering no more than the examination nerves with which Sara could sympathise. Perhaps the girl's eyes were too bright, her manner too restless, but outwardly she seemed to be in control, though her dependence on Rede's and Sara's approval of her performance was total.

'I believe you care more for Rede's opinion than you will for the judges,' Sara managed to tease her.

'Oh, but for yours too,' Mai bubbled. 'If I couldn't know you were both there, watching me, I should crumple, I know I should!' To which Sara, warmed against her will by such naïve enthusiasm, returned an emphatic, 'Rubbish!'

Apart from her chorus work, Mai had three assignments—a solo role of a princess, rescued by a knight from a horde of robbers to whom she was captive; a trio taper dance performed in darkness, but for the pattern of light made by the weaving movements of the girls' graceful hands, each finger elongated by a lighted taper fastened to it, and a mime in which a Buddhist girl bade farewell to her sweetheart, leaving her for his obligatory period of service as a monk.

'That is a very sad one,' Mai explained. 'They can hardly bear to part.'

'But it's only a matter of months for him, isn't it? The boy will be coming back?' Sara questioned.

'Oh yes. But the dance has also to show their fears of what may have happened for either or both of them before he comes back, and though the dancers may understand such fear, it is not easy to dance it to make other people feel it too,' explained Mai.

In the late afternoon Sara had an appointment with her hairdresser, who suggested that, to save her the trouble, he should dress the long fall of her hair into the high-piled style which she usually wore for formal evenings out with Rede. Lim had called for her by car and when she got into it, sitting beside him by choice, he handed her an oblong packet.

'For me, Lim? What is it?'

Lim shook his head. 'Tuan ask me to deliver it to you.'

Sara tore off the white paper wrapping. Inside was a jewellers' box and Rede's card. On a pad of black velvet inside the box lay a three-inch-long diamond bar-brooch, and Rede's card read, 'A memento of Mai's debut. Wear it, won't you?'

The diamonds sparked fire, Lim, seeing them, pursed his lips in admiration, then said, 'Apologies, mem, but they are very beautiful, are they not?' and Sara thought, Lovely ... but if only Rede did not send flowers by his florist and diamonds by his chauffeur, how much, much lovelier they would all be.

It was one of the busiest hours of the day for traffic. Long queues of cars and taxis formed at each intersection, and crawling to the next, met similar conditions there. It was at one such junction that as the lights turned to amber, a girl on a moped shot across the path of the car immediately ahead of Lim's. The car had the right of way and it sped on, the driver probably not aware that it had caught the moped a glancing blow. The girl swerved wildly, lost control of the machine and came down with a crash, the moped a mess of buckled handle-bars, whirring wheels and revving engine on top of her.

Pedestrians gathered about her. 'Heavens! Get out and see what we can do for her,' Sara ordered Lim, and got out herself.

Lim picked up the mangled moped. The girl had

been helped to her feet. As she stood shakily, brushing herself down while people clucked sympathy and advice over her grazed bare legs and hands, Sara recognised her instantly as Katin, George Merlin's temperamental 'cook'.

Sara touched her gently on the elbow. 'I know you, don't I? May I drop you anywhere by car?' she asked.

The beady eyes met hers in recognition. 'You don't have to,' Katin said in the English which Merlin had told Sara she could use very well when she chose.

'But please! Wherever you were going, you can't use your moped now. Look, there's a garage over there'—Sara pointed to it, 'so won't you let my chauffeur leave it there for you and we'll take you on in the car? Where do you want to go?'

Katin, bent double to examine a cut on her ankle, was understood to mutter, 'Home. To his place.'

'Mr Merlin's house, where I once came to lunch, you mean?'

A sulky nod. 'That's where.'

'Oh——' Fifteen miles out and fifteen back. Sara looked at her watch but calculated they could do it before she had to be ready for the concert. She sent Lim away with the machine and put Katin into the back seat of the car. For all Katin appeared to heed her advice about disinfecting and bandaging her cuts as soon as they reached the house, she might have been deaf. She sat in glum silence, and presently Sara gave up talking to her.

Before they arrived Sara asked if George Merlin

were likely to be at home, and when Katin said No, Sara went into the house with her, asking Lim to wait.

'First, your grazes. Hot water for bathing them—may I help you?' she asked. But Katin, ignoring her, marched straight into a bedroom, took an old-fashioned wicker holdall from a cupboard and began what looked like a thorough packing of her belongings.

Sara could only stare, bewildered. 'What now?' she asked.

'I am leaving,' said Katin.

'Leaving? For good? Before Mr Merlin comes home?'

'When he comes home I shall not be here. For when he does, he might beat me,' said Katin with dour candour.

'Rubbish!' scoffed Sara for the second time that day.

'And when he comes he will bring his new woman with him, and they will turn me out. So—I go first.' Katin finished scooping articles into the holdall, closed it, strapped it and took it up by the handle.

'But where do you propose to go? And how?' Sara asked.

'Home.'

'Really "home" this time? Where?'

'To my people. On the mainland.'

'Over the Causeway? But how? You haven't your moped now,' Sara reminded her.

Katin shrugged. 'I shall walk and——' she lifted

her thumb in a hitch-hike gesture.

'You'll do nothing of the kind! It'll be dark in less than an hour.' Sara calculated again. 'How far inland must you go?'

'Not far,' said Katin vaguely.

'Then we'd better take you on. But before you go, you're going to bathe those legs and hands, and I'll bandage them for you.'

With Katin obstructive, complaining that 'he' would come home, this took longer than it need, and when they went out to the car, Lim was dubious.

'Mem will be very late back,' he warned.

'I can't help that.' Privately Sara did not trust the girl not to resort to hitch-hiking, and she was not going to shoulder the responsibility of leaving her to it. After they had got under way, it occurred to her that they might have put Katin on a bus. But if it were indeed not far inland to her village, it did not seem worthwhile to do so now.

However, 'not far' was to prove the understatement of the year. Whenever they reached a junction in Johore and Lim would ask for directions, Katin would send him left or right or straight on, and it was only after nearly another hour's travelling along flat, dark roads bordered by rubber plantations that at a huddle of lighted houses, Katin announced that this was journey's end, and she was home.

Lim saw her into one of the houses, none of which appeared to have a telephone. Sara told Lim to stop at the first one they came to on the return journey. But here again was frustration. All lines to Singapore Island were temporarily engaged, and rather than wait indefinitely to tell Rede how late she was going to be, she decided to press on without stopping again.

A worried Buppa met her at the door. 'Tuan and Missee Kluai Mai gone nearly two hours,' she announced, 'Tuan say——'

'Yes, I know. I'm terribly late, and I've still got to change,' Sara cut in.

'Malee to help you, mem?' Buppa offered.

'It doesn't matter. At least my hair is done,' Sara said over her shoulder as she sped up the stairs, not realising that the elaborate effect created by her hairdresser was by now somewhat the worse for wear.

She was so hot and sticky that she couldn't resist taking a quick shower, and it was as she stepped back into her bedroom, clad only in a towel, that Rede came in.

She hadn't heard him knock, and one glance at his face warned her of his anger. She began breathlessly, 'I'm terribly sorry, but Buppa said you'd gone without me. Why have you come back?'

He countered icily, 'Why do you suppose? To see what had kept you, and whether you had any intention of attending Mai's concert before it was half over, or perhaps even at all!'

The very fact of his being handsome in tropical evening clothes and herself being nude under her towel put her more on the defensive than she need have been. 'Of course I meant to be there. I promised you, didn't I? And you sent me that exquisite brooch to remind me—as if I needed reminding! But what do you mean—"half over"? Mai hasn't danced her items yet, has she?'

Rede nodded. 'All of them before the intermission, which is on now. The second half is to be given over to ensembles and displays. But you knew that. Mai brought us a programme to see.'

'I didn't particularly notice the sequence of the items. And anyway, I couldn't help being as late as I was. There was an accident——'

'All right. Lim has filled me in on the details of your totally unnecessary dash up-island and then well into the interior of the mainland—all on behalf of a little tramp who probably asked for what she got, and could just as well have made her flit by bus!' Rede scoffed.

'If she is a tramp, it's because men like George Merlin have made her one,' retorted Sara, her anger rising. 'And when I saw she was afraid to stay to meet him and meant to leave him. I thought it was my duty to see her to her home.'

'There's a regular bus run to Johore Baru.'

'But not into the back of beyond where her home is. She would have walked or tried to hitch-hike—she'd said she would.'

'And so you put her needs into competition with Mai's, who is a good deal more deserving of your interest, I'd say.'

'But it just *happened* that way, and I haven't *withdrawn* any interest from Mai——!' Sara heard her voice turning shrill and stopped.

'Not even half-deliberately, in that though you didn't engineer this evening's misbegotten caper, you aren't too sorry that it happened?'

'Meaning that you suspect I'm not interested in seeing Mai do well?'

'Meaning that you're going to have to convince her that your intentions were of the best. She thought you understood how much she depended on you, and couldn't believe you'd let her down. She'd even laid on a surprise Malaysian dinner for us at the cottage beforehand, to which only I turned up.'

'I'm sorry,' Sara said, meaning it. She crossed the room to sit on her dressing-stool, saying undecidedly, 'I suppose there's no point in my coming to the concert now?'

'On the contrary, you're coming as soon as you're dressed. I've made enough excuses to your friends for your not being there, and we're taking Mai out to supper after the show.'

'I see. Then I'll hurry.' She expected him to leave the room to wait for her, but he remained where he was, and she hesitated about discarding the towel. Before she showered she had put her bra and evening slip and briefs handy, but she had never dressed from the nude in front of him and did not want to now.

'Throw me my wrap, will you?' she asked him.

'It's the lacy thing hanging inside the cupboard door.'

He did not move. 'Why? What are you afraid of?' he asked.

Facing the looking-glass, she saw her colour rise. 'Afraid of? Nothing,' she muttered.

'Then why the girlish modesty in front of me? I'm your husband—remember?' He moved forward then, plucked her bra from the chair where her things lay and came to stand behind her, waiting for her to drop the towel.

She did so and mutely offered her arms to the shoulder straps of the bra. He dealt deftly with its back fastenings and straightening, remarked, 'If you *were* afraid I might be harbouring thoughts of assault at the unexpected sight of your body, I'd mention that I've never yet attempted rape in a hurry. In which I am just now, and which you should be. So—all fears allayed, perhaps?'

Sara knew she had flushed again, this time less for shyness than with annoyance. 'I've told you, I wasn't afraid of anything,' she snapped. 'It's just that if I want privacy for dressing I think I'm entitled to it, and I'd have expected you could understand that. So now, my wrap—*please*?'

He fetched it for her and draped it round her shoulders where she sat. She snatched up her other things, took filmy tights from a drawer and marched past him to the bathroom. 'I hope to be with you in exactly five minutes,' she said, pretending she hadn't heard his laconic, 'A pity we're so pressed for time. Otherwise I believe I could have been tempted——' Pretending, in order to irk him, but needing to pretend to herself that his very lightest touch upon her skin hadn't a dark magic for her which she couldn't deny; needing to pretend that if they had opened for her, she wouldn't have gone, rapt, into his arms, her self-rightous anger no match for her love.

Meeting Isabel in the foyer during a later break in the programme, Sara realised she should have guessed what would be Isabel's reading of her earlier absence from the gala affair. And according to Isabel, not only hers, but that of several other people who had noted Rede's attendance alone and had wondered about it.

Isabel chanted with false brightness, 'So you did decide to come after all! Rather big-hearted of you, considering—Or did Rede have to twist your arm? Of course there could have been a dozen reasons why you didn't come with him to see his young friend doing her act, but I'm afraid we all thought we knew why, and rather pitied you—you know?'

For all her dismay, Sara feigned ignorance. Her brows lifted. 'Know what?' she enquired. 'Ought I to?'

'Ought to—what?'

'Know why you felt I was to be pitied?'

'Oh, my dear'—Isabel's tone held baffled patience—'do you need it spelled out *again*? Anyway, why do you suppose Ma Belmont is claiming she must find a boy-friend for Kluai Mai, if not because she likes you and thinks it might stop Rede from making a fool of himself over the girl?'

That shot went home, though in no way was Sara going to admit it. 'And if that were true of Rede, do you think I shouldn't know it?' she enquired.

'But would you? They say the injured party is always the last to hear.'

'Not,' Sara retorted, scoring a point of her own, 'when her so-called friends are only too anxious to be the first to tell her!'

Isabel lifted a shoulder. 'They do say too that there are none so blind——' she insinuated as Sara turned away.

When Mai came from backstage to join Rede and Sara in the car, she was laden with the bouquets which had been the tributes to her solo performance. She was bright-eyed and excited and far more ready to forgive Sara's absence than Rede had been. She showed her flowers with pride.

'See—these from you and Rede; and these from my dance-mistress, and these from the people in my class'— upon which Sara teased her,

'So you see, you didn't crumple as you threatened, just because only Rede was there to see you, did you? You didn't miss me at all!'

'But when I was on stage, I didn't know you weren't there. I thought——'

'You knew she hadn't come home in time for the meal you'd laid on for us,' Rede pointed out.

'Yes, but I knew she wouldn't let me down if she could help it. She had *promised*'—Mai turned anxious eyes upon him. 'You haven't made Sara feel badly about her not being there, have you?' she asked.

Rede's glance went to Sara. 'Tell the child, won't you, whether I beat you or not?' he invited her.

For Mai's sake, Sara forced a smile. 'It's all right. He didn't take a whip to me,' she said. (He only used the lash of his tongue to equal effect, was her unspoken reserve.)

'And he did tell you that I'd done well? Because somehow, once I began to dance, it didn't matter as much as I had expected, whether anyone—even you and Rede—was watching me or not. I just danced and forgot everything else. And I knew by the way people clapped and clapped the one with my—my lover, that I had made a success of it. So Rede did tell you all that, didn't he?' Mai appealed.

Rede hadn't. Sara remembered that she hadn't asked him, but he could have volunteered it, if he hadn't grudged her the satisfaction of hearing that her absence had affected Mai's performance not at all. How he must have needed to make her suffer a guilt for which only he blamed her! But the loyalty which was a part of love made her tell Mai, 'Oh yes—he was full of praise for how well you were doing,' and was rewarded by the quizzical look—of surprised gratitude?—which Rede threw her.

Mai ate very little, but she was still bright and volatile during the rest of the evening. When Rede dropped them both at the house and went to put away the car, she begged Sara, 'Come in with me, will you?' and Sara obeyed, unprepared for the electric change in the girl once the door of the cottage had closed upon them. Mai suddenly drooped—there was no other word for the limp sag of her body, reminding Sara of a mechanical toy lacking the turn of a key to keep it working.

Sara said with quick compassion, 'You're overtired——' To which Mai said, 'Yes,' and then 'No—not like that,' and sitting down at the table, leaned forward to it, her hands covering her eyes. Sara waited, then asked, 'What is it? You *are* tired, but you're unhappy too, when you should be riding on a pink cloud. So why aren't you? Do you feel you could tell me?'

A shake of Mai's head was her only reply, but after a minute, as if she had thought better of her denial of fatigue, she let her hands fall heavily into her lap and she sat up. 'Yes, that is it. I am tired, that's all.'

'No!' Sara rejected the evasion sharply. 'There's something else wrong, and there has been for some time. We've all noticed it and been worried for you. But if we hoped it was only that you were strung up about tonight, it seems we were wrong. Because though you've done all that was expected of you, the trouble is still there for you, isn't it?'

There was a dumb appeal in Mai's eyes as her lips formed, 'Yes.'

'Then what?' It had been in Sara's thought to

force the issue with the bald question, 'Is it because you and Rede have fallen in love with each
other, and you're guilty about it, because of me?'
But her courage failed her; she *couldn't* invite her
own doom so crudely, and she compromised with,
'Is it something to do with Rede—something he's
been, or said, or done to hurt you?' knowing only
too well, from the scene in the garden-room and
from Mai's abandoned letter to him, that it was
Rede who was at the root of her despair, as he
was of her own. Because of Rede, she and Mai
shared a common pain.

So that she would not have believed Mai if she
had said 'No' to the question. But she said 'Yes,'
and then enlarged on that with, 'Rede is so good.
But he expects so much ... too much, and when I
must fail him——'

'But you don't fail him, if you mean in your work.
Tonight, for instance, you couldn't have done better
than you did!'

Mai smiled wanly. 'That was a one-time, a—a sort
of peak. From there he will expect me to go on ...
and on, and do better and better. And when I care
so much about pleasing him, what if I cannot? As,
one day, I know I shall not.'

Was Mai only worried about her work? Remembering Ina Belmont's conviction that all she felt
for Rede was a teenage hero-worship, Sara took a
little heart, and felt she must brace her fears.

'You can't possibly know that,' she said. 'Rede
may expect you to go from success to success, but

there's no reason in the world why you shouldn't. Or can you think of one?'

There was a pause. Then Mai said, 'Yes, I know of one.'

'You do? What is it?'

But Mai shook her head. 'I cannot tell you. You would not understand,' she said.

'I see.' But all Sara saw was that in a few seconds the girl's stonewall reply had destroyed the accord between them. In face of that, she couldn't go on fencing with Mai. She left the argument there, and when Mai stood wearily and said she supposed she ought to go to bed, she agreed with her. They said goodnight, and impulsively Sara stooped to kiss Mai's cheek. But for the second time she left the cottage without knowing the truth about Mai and Rede.

CHAPTER SEVEN

SARA expected that she had seen the last of Katin after she had delivered the girl to her home on the mainland. But when on a morning's shopping trip she went into the restaurant of one of the big department stores for lunch, Katin was the waitress at her table.

'Well!' Sara smiled. 'Here's a surprise—do you remember me?'

Katin shook out a napkin and handed the menu

card. 'Of course,' she said woodenly.

'And you're working here now? You didn't'—Sara hesitated over the delicate question—'you didn't go back to Mr Merlin?'

The beady black eyes flashed. 'Go back there? To *that* one, when he throw me out after I cook for him for three—four year?' Katin demanded, with a convenient disregard of the truth of her parting from George Merlin. 'He owe me money—much money too,' she added.

'Well, you did walk out on him without notice, didn't you?' Sara felt it fair to remind her. 'How much money does he owe you, then?'

'Much. My wages. Things he tell me to get for the house and I pay for them. One hundred dollars—more.'

In Sara's opinion, twenty-five pounds or so in sterling wasn't too high a price to pay for independence of a man like George Merlin, but as she couldn't expect Katin to agree with her, she said inadequately, 'I'm sorry,' and changed the subject. 'But you have a good job here? You like it?'

Katin shrugged. 'Properly I am cook, not waiter on tables.'

Remembering cabbage-water soup and leathery veal, Sara doubted that. But she consoled, 'Well, perhaps when there is a vacancy in the kitchens, you can hope to be taken on there. Anyway, I'm glad you found another job so quickly.' She picked up the menu card. 'Shall I order now?'

But, her waitress role forgotten, Katin ignored

the suggestion. Avenging angel incarnate, she bent to Sara's ear. 'Never mind, I make him pay,' she muttered. 'Even if he not pay me, I make him one pile of trouble. For I *know* things about him, something that he tell me one time when he still like me. Something that I now tell to the police, and they go to work on him—boom!'

Sara stared up at her, frowning. 'You mean—something criminal? And you've already told the police?'

Straightening again, Katin nodded. 'Any time now you will hear of it—in the *Straits Times*—all over!'

'But what? We shall hear—what?'

'All that I tell the police. That he sends out drugs in his crates of orchids. Just in one box or two in every hundred, and he laugh a lot that he so get away with it. And if anyone ask questions, he withdraw the boxes and sends out no drugs in that lot. Or he can blame the man who sign out the shipment. That man, he will say, has slipped in the drugs himself. *He* know nothing about it, and so he will simply fire the man and let the police have him.'

Instantly Sara's thoughts flew to what Isabel had told her about Cliff's new job. 'And has he ever done that, do you know? Got rid of anyone in that way?' she asked Katin.

But Katin hadn't heard, she said. It was, she thought, only what Merlin planned to do if suspicion fell on him. 'And it will,' she threatened darkly. '*I* have seen to that.'

Sara was appalled, wishing she could dismiss the story as the vindictive revenge of the man's cast-off mistress. But if Katin had already approached the police, she must have believed she had substance to her accusations, and *if* she had, Sara saw the consequences for Cliff as wholly disastrous. Either Merlin had taken Cliff into league with him, or he intended to use him as his catspaw. It was as hideously simple as that, and little sympthy as she had with Cliff, he should be protected from the results of his trust in Merlin.

'And what did the police say when—?' she began. But with a glance across the restaurant at the handsome young Malay in Western head waiter's dress, Katin was again a waitress, adjusting the table cutlery while she waited for Sara's order.

'He is watching me, the maître d'hôtel,' she whispered, her lips scarcely moving. 'So choose, please, madame, if you will.'

Sara glanced herself at the young man, immobile, but obviously very watchful of his domain. 'That man?' she smiled at Katin. 'He doesn't look old enough to be a head waiter.'

'He is not. He is only assistant. But he is new and very correct, and if he thinks I gossip with you, madame——'

'Of course.' Sara obliged by giving her attention to the menu and ordering.

While she ate, she debated what could possibly be done for Cliff if Katin's story were true. Isabel, she guessed, would never forgive him if he were even remotely connected with anything so shady, and if he were actually involved——! She had no more friendly brief for Isabel than she had for Cliff, but she dared not let him go blind into trouble which might be prevented if she acted in time; acted with the help of the only person to whom she could turn—Rede.

She turned cold at the thought of pleading Cliff's case with Rede, after her hot denial that Cliff meant anything to her. At the time she had persuaded herself that Rede had believed her. But supposing he had not, what was he going to conclude from her support for Cliff now? Was there any way to avoid telling Rede what she had heard? *Was* there? She had found none by the time Katin brought her bill to her table and when that happened the young head waiter was there too, asking if she had enjoyed her meal, thanking her for her patronage and politely bowing her away, giving Katin no further chance to speak to her. As she left the restaurant the passing thought occurred to her that his wordless control of his staff and his manner and poise would probably take him a long way in his profession. Then she forgot him in the urgency of the problem which Katin had wished on her.

She worried at it all day and took it to Rede that evening, plunging in on the telling until he stopped her, his response to it unreadable from his expression.

'And what's your interest in this scandal?' he wanted to know.

So far she hadn't mentioned Cliff's name, but now she had to. 'Well, Cliff,' she said. 'That's his job with George Merlin, Isabel says—responsibility for checking consignments before they're shipped, and if Katin isn't lying about the whole thing, then Merlin could——'

'She isn't lying,' put in Rede flatly.

Sara stared at him. 'You know she isn't? How?'

'Never mind. But she's not the only one to have tattled to the police, and they've had a suspicious eye on Merlin Enterprises for some time. They intend to act, I believe. Probably in a surprise raid at the point of despatch, or at the other end, when the stuff tries to pass Customs.'

Sara gave a long sigh. Among her worries had been the fear that, caught, Merlin might remember Katin as his likeliest betrayer and try to deal with her accordingly. She told Rede so and took some reassurance from his, 'At that stage, I doubt if he'll have much opportunity for wreaking revenge.'

'But suppose he gets wind of trouble before then, as she thinks he may?' Sara pressed.

'As a willing and eager informer on him, she's probably prepared to risk that—even getting a thrill from the chance he gave her to play traitor to him. Revenge is always very sweet'—Rede paused. Then, 'But that's the point at which *your* headache begins, isn't it?' he challenged. 'Where, the girl suggests, Merlin boasts that he can get out from under by incriminating a scapegoat—Iden?'

Sara nodded dumbly.

'I'd be right in concluding that the whole object in your running to me with the story is your concern that pitch shouldn't touch him?'

She had to admit that her first impulse of alarm had been for Cliff. 'I suppose so—largely,' she said.

'As if I couldn't guess!'

Rede's tone was edged with the ice she had feared when Cliff's name had to come up, but she went on, 'Well, *shouldn't* I have hoped that you could see the danger for him too?'

'And that, seeing it, I should dash to his rescue on the nod? For the sake of the old times you and he had shared, perhaps? Or even in the name of his current yen for you—who knows?' Rede scoffed.

'That you might do *something*, yes,' she returned steadily. 'I trusted you to know what might be possible, and I did think you could care enough for his reputation and for Isabel's at least to warn him against George Merlin on what we know.'

'Why me? I'm sure he would prefer you to do any warning!'

Sara ignored the gibe. 'There's another thing. Both he and Isabel have people—Cliff, elderly parents in England, and Isabel relatives here too. So if Cliff gets implicated for want of a warning he could be given, what about them?' she demanded.

'So—what about them?' Rede echoed.

'Don't you care then about how much they could be hurt if Cliff gets into trouble?'

'Enough.' Rede's lips snapped shut on the word before he repeated it. 'Enough to see that, if it isn't already too late, Iden gets his warning. After that, it's his scene and his problem. Well?'

'If you mean am I satisfied that you will do what you can—yes. And thank you,' Sara said.

'Yes, well—I meant rather more than that. As well as your gratitude, I'd like your assurance that in asking my help, you aren't casting me in the role of tame cuckold to Iden?'

Sara flinched at the stark word. Had he been within reach, she would have been tempted to strike him. But he was yards away; she could picture the shame of his warding off her hand as she raised it, and her only weapons were words.

'How dare you imply that Cliff is my lover?' she raged. 'All right—you may have thought you had reason to think it on one occasion. But I told you then, and I'm repeating it now—he means nothing to me. *Nothing*, do you hear?'

'And, dupe or not as I may have been, I believed you then.'

'But not now? Not *now*—just because I plead for a man we both know, who meant a great deal to me—once, and who's in trouble? A man with a wife who, for all I know, may have been more than "just good friends" with *you*? Dupe indeed! You suspect I was lying then and you think it still, because you can't believe that, without wanting to see either of them again, I can care what happens to them——?'

She broke off, spent with her own vehemence, and from the long look with which Rede studied her, she took a little heart that she had convinced him at last. But when he spoke all he had for her was a pseudo-reasonable, 'You almost persuade me—if not quite. For you see, I can't forget that your emotions have never been tepid where Iden is concerned.'

'They were tepid, if not stone cold, as soon as he jilted me!'

Rede shook his head. 'Not "as soon as". Even when I came along, they were hot and steamy and vengeful enough to make you willing to put any man's ring on your finger, in order to prove to Iden that you could.'

'I might have expected you to bring that up,' Sara muttered.

'Why not? It was my first glimpse of your fury at his rejection of you, and your passionate plea for him, now that you have him at your feet again, could well be the other side of the same coin, the same infatuation.'

'He is *not* at my feet! He jilted me for Isabel and he loves her.'

'Does he? Considering his continuing interest in you, I'd only believe that if he told me so. Or if Isabel ever wore the air of a happily fulfilled wife, which she doesn't.'

'Well, it's not Cliff's fault if she isn't one, and you've said yourself that she's discontented by nature. And if you were really as jealous of him as you sound, you couldn't wait to find out from him whether he still wants me or not. But of course'— Sara paused to gather the full forces of her scorn— 'you aren't jealous of me in any red-blooded, common human way. It's only your pride of possession of merchandise that you bought and paid for that you're defending, isn't it?'

For a frightening moment Rede allowed her to see the naked anger in his eyes. Then, after a swift lowering of his lids, it was gone. Then he countered, 'And if only fish-cold blood runs in my veins, why do you suppose I promised you I'd do what I could to warn Iden of his danger?'

Sara thought. Why had he? At last she said, 'I don't know.'

'And perhaps you think I didn't mean it?'

'No. You promised, and I'm sure you will.'

'Good. I'm grateful for that crumb of faith.' The slight dip of his head was an ironic bow in her direction. 'But if you're quite blind as to why, what about considering I may have done it in self-interest?'

'Self-interest? Yours?'

'Mine. Iden came out here on my recommendation and on my judgment of him as a good man for the job. In the long term, given his goodwill, I could have shaped him for it and been right. But in the short term I was wrong, and it isn't going to do anything for either my self-esteem or my reputation if he's to be branded and hounded as a criminal's yes-man. Do you see?'

Sara said slowly, 'I suppose so. You're afraid that the pitch—the mud or whatever—mightn't cling only to him?'

Rede nodded. 'A possible reason for my co-operation, wouldn't you say? Or even a probable one, perhaps?'

'Yes,' she agreed. 'And more than probably your only one, since you wouldn't have considered doing it because I asked it of you—for Cliff.'

When he said nothing to that, she left him standing and went out of the room.

'*Not for me. Not for me!*' her heart was crying. Nothing ever for her, but what he, in his arrogant ownership of her, chose to give. That night, she expected that he might come to her to insist on his rights, as he had done before.

But after that scene he did not visit her room again.

Before the police had perfected their case against George Merlin, rumour had begun to walk and talk. It was the gossip of the bars and the restaurants and the clubs that all was not well with Merlin Enterprises, but speculations as to its trouble were vague. The police kept a low profile, and no accurately accusing finger was pointed at its chief until Cliff, warned and acting as decoy, was able to report that George Merlin had personally ordered two marked boxes of orchids to be withdrawn from a particular consignment for Europe.

Cliff withdrew them; turned them over to the

police, waiting on such a chance for weeks; both crates were found to be carrying illicit drugs in tiny concealed compartments—proof that Merlin's guilt of the traffic was only too real.

But evidently he had his own active spies. He had gone too far, risked too much, and his scapegoat, Cliff, was already on the side of the enemy. But before a warrant was issued for his arrest, he disappeared. One day he was there; the next he was not, irrevocably lost to justice in some haunts of Asia or Europe or North Africa to which no doubt he had planned to repair, in the unlikely events which had overtaken him. His creditors moved in like vultures; his business kingdom folded almost overnight, leaving the field of the export of orchids wide open to his new competitors, Temasik. For his many field workers and his staff his collapse was traumatic, and while for many of the former there would presently be work with Temasik, there was no room in the Temasik offices for any more executive personnel—among whom of course Cliff was one.

Sara knew from Rede that Cliff's help had been co-opted by the police, but apart from that she learned only the barest details of Rede's manoeuvres on Cliff's behalf, and she suspected he would have kept from Cliff the satisfaction of hearing that she was concerned for him. Even when the case against Merlin broke wide open, Rede hardly discussed it with her, treating it as news in which he was not over-involved.

During those weeks she thought they were farther apart than they had ever been in the months of their marriage. Her body might ache for his, but in her heart there was a stone of hurt resentment of a withdrawal from her which she knew she did not deserve.

Resolved against bringing up Cliff's name again with him, she was left to speculate on how Isabel was taking Cliff's loss of his job on the collapse of George Merlin's empire. Isabel, Sara felt sure, would conveniently forget that it was she who had pushed Cliff into resigning from Temasik, and how was she going to react to his complete loss of prospects now? It was odd, Sara reflected, how her own fiery resentment of Cliff's jilting and her sick jealousy of Isabel of only a few months ago had wisped away like smoke. Neither of them could hurt her now. That power had switched to Rede's mistrust and contempt of her, both of which, he had brutally claimed, she had invited.

People said of the Idens that they would probably go back to England, where Isabel's father might pull strings for Cliff. Others had it that Isabel was threatening to leave Cliff, to stay indefinitely with her Singapore relatives. But on both counts the gossips had got it wrong when Isabel announced to Sara in some triumph that Cliff was returning to Temasik at Rede's invitation.

To say the least, Sara was surprised. Even this move Rede had not seen fit to confide to her! But pretending to know all about it, she frowned, as if searching her memory.

'Let's see, *did* Rede tell me Cliff was to get his old job back or not?' she mused aloud.

'He's being promoted!' Isabel returned sharply.

'Ah yes, now I remember'—Sara murmured sagely. But Isabel was quick to detect a flaw in her ruse.

'If Rede told you he'd begged Cliff to join Temasik again, surely he must have told you as well that he's promoting Cliff—to the Hong Kong branch?' Isabel demanded.

Sara had to shake her head. 'No, really?' she queried. 'Hong Kong? That must have been a later decision which Rede hasn't had time to tell me about.'

'Any more, at a guess, than he's bothered to tell you how desperate he was to get Cliff back?' Isabel challenged.

This was more than Sara was prepared to take. 'Was he? Rede, I mean—desperate? Now that's odd—when I remember he once told me he'd made a business mistake in bringing Cliff out here at all!'

She had made her point. 'You're lying!' Isabel almost spat, and then fired her parting shot, 'Because if Rede hasn't any use for Cliff, why has he taken him back at all?'

She didn't wait for an answer, but Sara couldn't care that there was none she could have given. For the news of Rede's dismissal of Cliff and Isabel to the thousand-mile distance and comparative obscurity of the small Hong Kong office was music to her ears and enough stimulus to her spirit to tell him when they met, 'I hear from Isabel Iden that you're sending her and Cliff north to Hong Kong?'

'Yes,' said Rede.

'Why?'

'Because their removal seemed the best solution to a problem.'

(She *wouldn't* concede that Cliff was any problem between herself and him, which she guessed was what he meant.) 'What problem?' she asked aloud.

He looked straight at her, through her. 'You should know,' he said. 'We've lived with it long enough.'

That told her nothing. But she hadn't expected anything less than cryptic words from him. As she had dared to taunt him, he couldn't know what impassioned jealousy was, when he was only concerned to guard from Cliff a wife he had taken in cool calculation of her use to him and and whom he had treated with the minimum of tenderness since. No— he had simply rid himself of the nuisance value of Cliff as he would have despatched any other business problem. There was, she was convinced, no more troubled heart to his jealousy of Cliff than that.

Now Rede's frequent absences from home, in Thailand or on the mainland, linking what was left of Merlin's export business to Temasik's new traffic in orchids, had the effect of her finding a certain companionship with Mai, and Mai seeming to find the same with her. Perhaps it was because they shared the same reason for missing him—because they both loved him, Sara thought wistfully, or perhaps because, when he was not there, they were free to indulge in easy woman-talk without any undercurrents of tension running between them.

Mai continued to do some advanced work at the dance school, and though she did not seem as anxious as she had been to take some pupils, she was now getting some professional engagements, and was saving, she told Sara, towards paying her own way.

Often she and Sara now ate together, and she taught Sara many Malaysian and Chinese dishes in return for Sara's demonstration of Western ones. But their friendship remained on that undemanding level; whenever their talk verged upon the personal, Sara sensed Mai's withdrawal. She would change the subject, giving Sara no chance to probe whatever trouble had brought her to the despair of those abandoned efforts to write to Rede.

Only once during that time did Sara catch a glimpse of her with a man. That was on one morning when Sara was again leaving the store where Katin worked, and saw Mai ahead of her, wheeling her bicycle and walking beside a young Malay. They parted at a street corner, Mai riding away on her machine and her companion having disappeared on a side street by the time Sara reached the corner

herself. She felt a little frustrated. Without being
able to place him, she had a vague idea she had
recognised his back view. But when Mai did not
mention him, nor did she, having by now reluctantly accepted Mai's barriers to her private life.

It was when she had done some small purchases
for Mai and had taken them to the cottage that
she was to realise how mistaken that indulgence had
been. She knew Mai had no classes that morning
and she expected to find her at home. But when
there was no answer to her knock, Sara noticed that
the key was in the unlocked door, and walked in.

She halted in the bright living-room and called
a greeting which was answered by silence. She
looked about her at a strange difference in the room,
a neat emptiness caused by the absence of all Mai's
personal things—her books, the two or three silk
panels which she had hung upon the walls, her
vase of joss-sticks, and most noticeable void of all,
the gilt Buddha image before which she laid a tri-
bute of a single flower every morning.

No flower. No Buddha. That told its unbelievable
story, as did Mai's bedroom, stripped of her clothes,
her luggage bags and her toilet articles. Mai had
gone, leaving the cottage as denuded of herself as
she had found it. Gone, this time without begging
Rede's permission to escape—but where?

Sara wandered back into the living-room, noticing now on the table a bulging envelope addressed
to Rede. Surely a very long letter to him? Recalling the details of their ill-starred affair? Telling

him where she had fled to? Asking his forgiveness, as she had tried to do before; pressing her right to retreat from an impossible situation? Or what?

Sara relocked the cottage door and took the letter with her back to the house. She rang Rede at his office and asked to be put through to him urgently. He came on the line. 'What is it? What's the matter?' he asked.

She told him. 'And the letter? What does it say?' he wanted to know.

'I don't know—I haven't opened it. It's addressed to you,' Sara told him.

'Tcha! What of it? Open it now and read it out to me——' He checked. 'Or no—better not, over the phone. Read it yourself, and I'll come back at once. Meet me at Mai's place and keep Buppa and the staff away from it at the moment.' He rang off.

Sara opened the letter with fingers that shook. What was it going to tell her about Rede and Mai? Her knees were shaking too as she sat down on Mai's couch to read it.

It wasn't a long letter at all. The bulk of the package was a thick wad of dollar notes which she didn't count. The letter, on a single sheet, explained that they were in part payment for Mai's tuition and keep; all she had been able to save to date. For the rest there were two short sentences.

'Please, Rede, do not try to find me. You will hate me for what I have done to you, and this I could not bear to see.'

That was all. But to Sara's reading of it, it told her all she had been afraid to know. For what could possibly cause Rede to 'hate' Mai, but her guilty desertion of his love?

Before Rede came to her, Sara's fingers had creased and pleated the letter into a spill as narrow as a wax taper. She wished she could use it as one.

CHAPTER EIGHT

REDE noticed the roll of notes on the table as soon as he came in.

'What's this?' he asked, picking it up.

'She explains here.' Sara smoothed out Mai's letter and gave it to him.

He read it, frowning, then looked up. 'And what does this mean to you?' he asked.

'Well, that she wants the money to free her of some obligation to you——'

'Obviously. But the rest?'

Sara's mouth went dry. 'Much the same as it does to you, I suppose,' she managed.

Rede snapped, 'It means nothing comprehensible to me, except that she's done a moonlight flit and has the nerve to expect we'll let her go without a trace. But to you?'

'To me'—Sara paused to choose her words—'it

means that she knows the wrong she's done you by running away, but that she can't live with her conscience any longer by staying.'

'And so she should have a conscience over such a low-down trick!' Rede exploded.

'You've misunderstood me. I think you've misunderstood Mai. She's telling you that she can only finish with the guilt she's suffering *by* running away. From you,' Sara added with a meaning which he must surely understand.

If he did, he gave no sign. 'From me?' he echoed. 'Why from me in particular?'

Watching him, Sara could not tell whether his blankness was a true innocence of an affair with Mai or whether his quick thinking was using it as a front while he played for time. She remembered her spoken scorn of Isabel for not being able to trust her husband. But here was she herself, not only doubting the fidelity, but dreading the defensive subterfuges of her own. She said reluctantly, 'Because she's in love with you, and she has enough conscience to be unhappy—for me.'

What she expected him to reply to that she did not know, and he kept her guessing for some seconds. Then he scoffed, 'In love with me—rubbish! And even if she imagined she was, how could the calf love of a girl like her affect you, my wife?'

'She might think it could.' Sara knew that moral courage should have added,—'if she knew that you loved her in return,' and have steeled itself to his honest reply to that. But her voice refused to frame the words; she longed to cling, for as long as he would let her, to her fool's paradise of hope that his rejection of Mai was as sincere as it sounded, and when he answered his own question with a brisk, 'No! There has to be some better reason for her decamping than some imaginary personal hurt to me or to you,' Sara let it ride. If Rede didn't volunteer the truth—supposing he was hiding it now—then she wouldn't trap him into it. Her pride couldn't stoop so far.

Flicking the roll of notes with a fingernail, he went to stand with his back to her at the window.

'It could be an exaggerated idea about the money. That she's taken more of what she calls "charity" from us than she thinks is right,' he mused, thinking aloud.

Sara said, 'No, it's more than that. She's got that off her back by returning to you as much money as she could. She says so.'

'Mm.' He accepted the argument with a nod.

'And she's been unhappy about—something since before her debut concert. You know that,' Sara reminded him.

'That was cold feet, nerves, butterflies in the tum—nothing to run away from, once she'd done well, and she did. And she's been working as hard as ever since then.'

'Has she?' Sara stopped short of 'How do you know?' for that was a trap.

'Well, hasn't she?' Rede retorted. 'You should know?'

'Yes, but——'

He swung about. 'And here are we, chewing over the whys and wasting good time, instead of looking for the hows and the wheres—particularly the wheres. For pity's sake *think*,' he demanded of Sara. 'Where could she have gone, hoping not to be found?'

Sara thought, without much reward. 'Home to the mainland?' she offered, unhelpfully she knew.

Rede shook his head. 'The first place she would know we should look.'

'But could you telephone to find out?'

'Suchee and Yuki-Ling aren't on the phone. But yes, I'll ring the police at Kota Tingii and ask them to go round to the bungalow to see if Mai is there.'

'If she only left this morning, could she be there yet?'

'Assuming luck with connecting buses, pretty well, or soon. But it's a forlorn hope. And more ideas? What friends did she ever bring back with her here?'

'Not many. A few dancers from the School, that's all.'

'Girls or boys or both?'

'Always girls.' (With Rede as the sun in her sky, was Mai likely to have brushed more than acquaintance with many of the men dancers she met? thought Sara.)

'Well, we can ask at the School about her—the last class she attended, who were her friends, get their names and addresses.'

'Would you ask the police here to post her as a missing person?'

'At this stage? Good heavens, no. We'd have reporters and busybodies around our ears like wasps.' Rede moved towards the door. 'Anyway, the police at Kota Tingii first and then the School—want to come with me?' he offered.

'Please,' said Sara.

They had to give the Kota Tingii police time to visit the bungalow of Mai's foster-parents and to ring back with the result. At the Dance School they learned that Mai had attended her yesterday's classes as usual, but had not appeared for that morning's. The principal denied knowledge of any trouble at the School which could have caused Mai to leave and two girl students who she knew to be Mai's friends could not help either.

Rede and Sara were back at the house in time to take the police call saying that Mai had not gone to her home, nor had been seen on any arriving bus. After that, short of making her disappearance public, which Rede insisted on delaying, there seemed nothing more to be done. He went back to his office; he had a business dinner to attend that night, and he would be leaving early to fly to Bangkok the next day. Sara spent the rest of her day restlessly between the house and the cottage, seeking there some clue which Mai might have overlooked. Rede had told Buppa that Mai had been called home unexpectedly and Sara had to play along with this. In the evening she dined early from a tray and went to bed, not waiting for Rede to return.

She couldn't sleep for her churning thoughts, worrying about Mai, blaming Mai, pitying Mai; doubting Rede, believing in Rede; knowing herself for the coward she had been in not having forced him to admit or to deny his part in the despair which had caused Mai to break free of whatever it was that she feared from their continued association. Just one question had been needed, and Sara hadn't asked it.

She heard him come in, and expected he would knock to see if she were awake and had anything to report. But evidently concluding she had not, he went to his own room and presently all was quiet there.

After that she must have dozed a little, but shortly was wide awake again. This was impossible! Mosquitoes or no, she had to have air. She got out of bed, pulled on a chiffon negligee and went out on to the balcony to meet a pungency in her nostrils and to see a silhouetted figure, lighted by the glow of a cigar, leaning on the rail—Rede.

'Oh——!' She drew back into the wall-shadow.

He turned, saw her and beckoned her to the rail. 'What's the matter?' he asked.

'I haven't been able to sleep, and I craved some air.'

'Same here.' He drew on the cigar and indicated it. 'Do you mind?'

'No. You know I like it.'

'It should keep the bugs away at least. Has there

been any news? Anything happened?'

'Nothing.'

'I guessed not, or you would have waited up to tell me.'

'Of course.'

Close, forearm to forearm on the rail, they looked out over the sleeping but still brightly lit city. Sara wondered if Rede could hear the pounding of her heart as she could, and suddenly knew what she had to say.

'Rede——?' He turned her way. 'Rede—about Mai. When you read her letter, you claimed you didn't know why she's run away. You—pretended to look for reasons; you questioned me, and the people we saw, as if we might know, while you hadn't a clue yourself. But you do know, don't you? Or you've guessed?' She paused. 'Please—you owe me the truth.'

He did not answer directly. 'You think you have the right idea—that she's made something romantic out of my interest in her, and has worked up a guilt complex in consequence?' he asked.

Not looking at him, 'Yes, and more than that.'

'More? How much more?'

Sara drew a long breath. 'Just that—on her side. That she's in love with you. But on yours, that you know it and you've encouraged her because you— you love her in return.'

'And so?' Ash from his cigar glowed momentarily and died.

'And so'—Sara took up the non-committal

phrase—'being good, and with a conscience and unhappy because, though she had begged you, you wouldn't let her go, she had to act for herself. And this—her running away—is what she's done.'

Rede murmured, 'Mm, interesting. And how do you know—or think you know—that she felt she had to escape from me?'

Sara told him.

He listened in silence. 'And so, from a private letter which she hadn't even finished and which certainly I never received, you concluded that she wanted out from a clandestine affair with me, but that—hypnotised by me, no doubt!—she abandoned the idea of getting away until now?' He stopped Sara's attempt to speak with an imperious lift of his hand, and went on, 'And supposing I told you I've never thought of nor touched Kluai Mai in any way of love, what would you say to that—self-wronged wife of mine?'

She had to moisten her dry lips. 'I'd want very badly to believe you,' she said.

'Why?' The curt question sprang at her as dangerously as a flicked-open knifeblade. 'Wh-what do you mean—why?' she faltered.

'I'm asking what it matters to *you* whether or not I'm double-crossing you with another woman—which for the definitive record I am not. Or in other words, even if I were, what have you got to lose?'

She looked in bewilderment at the dark shape that was his face. 'I—am your wife, after all,' she reminded him.

'My wife, I agree. But in what way, except the
way you wanted marriage and got it, which in my
view would give you no right to a sense of high
grievance against me, even if I deceived you with
a dozen "little friends" every week?' he demanded
savagely, then conceded, 'All right, I admit your
loss of status, once the gossips knew. But if I saw to
it that you didn't suffer that, how much betrayed
passion for me *could* you claim? How much woun-
ded love? How much blighted loyalty—hm?'

If he had really wanted an answer to that, Sara
could have let him read it in an ardent abandon-
ment to his arms, his lips, his virile body which
she dared not contemplate. For he only meant to
taunt her. He had already decided she had brought
as little warmth to their marriage as he had, and
as to that she could retort in kind.

'As I remember, your terms of marriage didn't
expect love from me and didn't offer any to me.
You found yourself with "a use for marriage", you
said. It suited you to marry me, or you wouldn't
have asked me. And of course one use I filled for
you was to play chaperone to Mai,' she said.

'If that was all I wanted, I could have employed
a duenna for her,' Rede pointed out.

'Who, I daresay you're thinking now, might have
looked after her better!' she flung at him.

He shrugged. 'Who would have been a mere paid
servant, not the companion I hoped you would be
for Mai, and she for you. But that aside, I do have
other uses for a wife.' He paused. 'As I thought I'd

demonstrated,' he added with a significance she knew he meant she should take.

She felt her anger surge. 'Uses, yes! And rights of possession! And payment extorted for bed and board and the sharing of your name—all those!' she sneered, her voice rising, out of control.

'*And* the right to deal with the tantrums of an hysterical child in the time-honoured way of sending it to bed,' Rede said quietly, shaming her outburst. He had discarded his cigar and now turned her inward towards him, but at arm's length.

On the verge of nervous tears, 'I'll go back to bed when I'm ready!' she defied him.

'You'll go now.' He swept her up, one arm beneath her knees, another behind her shoulders, and carried her into her bedroom where he set her down with no more care than he might have given to any load of her size and weight. While she kicked off her mules and dropped her negligee, he smoothed the bed and when she was in it, pulled the covers over her.

'I can't sleep to order,' she said petulantly.

'If you relax and lie still, you will in time,' he assured her.

She sat up, resting on an elbow. 'You couldn't sleep either,' she reminded him.

'That was for a different reason than that I'd worked myself up into a lather of temper.' Ready to switch off the bedside light, he pressed her back on to her pillow. 'Try,' he said, and as the light flicked out she felt his lips brush across her own before he left her to the longing and regret which flooded over her.

He had never yet kissed her so gently, with so little demand of her response. He had made it a conciliatory kiss for a peevish child, and that in itself was a rebuke. But he had been there—close— within reach of arms which ached to open to him. If she had clung to his kiss, invited him with the warmth of hers, drawn him down to her, might he perhaps have stayed long enough for her to try to express all that her body and spirit, hungry for him, wanted to tell him?

Supposing, reckless, she had pleaded, 'I love you,' would he believe it meant what it said and be kind? Or would confession of her need of him put her even more into the power of his intolerance, add pity for her to the contempt he already had?

Anyway, she hadn't kept him with her, and the might-have-beens of her having dared it, she would never know.

She woke to the heaviness following late sleep after a wakeful night. There was a note from Rede on her breakfast tray. He had already left to fly to Bangkok, but he gave an address where he could be reached in case there was news of Mai. The note was written on a page torn from a diary; he must have sent it back by Lim, who would have driven him to the airport.

Most of the day Sara waited, for what to happen she didn't know. Perhaps for Mai to appear or to

ring, or for Rede to call to check for any news, or—
pretty vainly—for some idea or clue to occur to
her, which she could look into on her own.

There was nothing; no Mai, no calls, no ideas,
until the late afternoon when, lying on a sunlounger
in the garden, she shot bolt upright, almost shouting to the garden stillness, 'Yes!' and again, 'Yes—
Now I know——' for memory and instinct told her
she did.

Mai, according to her girl friends, never known
to have dated a man or invited him to the cottage,
had been seen once with a man, seen walking with
him by Sara herself, and what was more, Sara knew
him, had recognised him from only one sighting
of him before.

A small enough chance that he had had any part
in Mai's disappearance, but with it as the only
chance, Sara was already making plans.

They meant a journey into the city to contact
Katin. For Katin and the store where she worked
were the leads to Mai's friend—the handsome young
Malay, Katin's urbane deputy-chief of the store's
restaurant, who on a certain morning had parted
from Mai at the corner of the store block, to vanish
within minutes on a long straight side street as if
he had been spirited away.

But Sara, remembering, realised there had been
no magic to it. Employed by the store, he would
have returned to work by a staff entrance, and Sara's
first errand in the city would be to look for such
an entrance in that street. Then she would go in

search of Katin; find out the man's name and ask
permission to speak to him. At last there was something she could *do*; something, however trivial, she
could report to Rede.

She decided against taking Lim. She would go
by taxi to the store and hope she would leave it,
armed with some clue as to where Mai might be—
an errand which might take her further afield—or
not, if the scent she was on was dead or had never
existed except in her imagination. But at least to
try was to do something for Rede.

The store's staff entrance proved to be where she
had expected it to be. The young man could easily
have reached it before she had looked along the
street herself. She went into the store by the main
doors, took the lift to the restaurant and looked
around for Katin.

She was not there, nor was the Malay waiter. The
store did not serve dinners, and with the lunch hour
long over, the only customers were two ladies for
afternoon tea, attended by one waitress, whom Sara
approached when she was free.

It was Katin's day off, the girl said. The deputy
head waiter was also on a week's holiday. No, she
did not know Katin's address, but the store's personnel officer would help Madam, no doubt. 'On the
next floor, madam—the executive offices; ask for
Mrs Sunderabad,' she advised.

Sara thanked her. On her way to Mrs Sunderabad's office, she realised with dismay that she herself knew Katin's home to be far inland in Johore.

But Mrs Sunderabad a be-saried Malaysian woman with perfect English, pooh-poohed the idea that Katin commuted to work from so far away, and gave Sara an address in Chinatown where Katin lodged with her married sister.

So far, so good. Sara picked up another taxi and gave the driver the paper on which Mrs Sunderabad had written Katin's address. He nodded and set off for the teeming streets of Chinatown, threading at speed through their mazes whenever the way was clear and exchanging gestures and raucous jokes with his fellows whenever, as frequently happened, an evening market intermittently obstructed the traffic of a whole street length.

Katin's sister lived on one such street, in a tall tenement house with canary cages hung from the upper balconies and items of household linen draping the rails of the lower ones. The number Sara wanted proved to be the ground-floor apartment and at her knock a young woman appeared with a black-eyed toddler on either side of her.

Sara began to explain in careful English that she was looking for Katin Char who, she believed— She got no further. The young mother backed from the door and called into the house, 'Katin!' followed by a chatter in Malay of which 'Mem' was the only word Sara understood.

Katin came out; her sister did not reappear; the babes remained, a thumb in each pouting mouth, sometimes staring at Sara, sometimes at the garish stall at the curbside behind her. Sara explained her errand without going into details; she rather particularly wanted to know the name of Katin's deputy chief in the restaurant, and perhaps, if Katin knew, where he lived.

Surprisingly incurious, Katin said, 'His name is Charn Narong. He live in Changi village, I do not know where.'

Sara knew the place for a Government-sponsored small model town not far from the city, a kind of garden suburb laid out round a shopping precinct and with a batik factory to provide employment. But how to find one Charn Narong in even so small a place?

However, she thanked Katin for knowing even so much about him, and asked, 'Is he a married man, do you know?'

Katin thought not, he lived with his parents, she volunteered, and added. 'He is Buddhist. When he come as waiter, he is only just out of his service as monk.'

'A monk? I see.' Sara knew of the religion's rule that its young men must serve a minimum period of five months as religious mendicants, begging alms and their food and 'touching no woman' during their service. 'And about when did he come to the restaurant?' she asked.

Katin shrugged. 'Two months?' she offered, and then was interested enough to ask, 'How do you find where I live now?'

Sara told her. At which Katin began, 'And if you

ask Mrs Sunderabad about me, why do you not ask her where——?'

The question was never finished in the crisis of the next few fraught minutes. Sara was aware that, behind her, the stallholder had been keeping both the children spellbound with his juggling of a papaya fruit the size of a football. But as Katin was speaking he dropped it.

It bounced to the roadway with a thump. The man scrambled for it and tripped. One of the toddlers darted, shouting with glee—straight into the path of a motor-cyclist weaving a reckless course through the more cumbrous traffic.

For a stricken moment of inaction Sara stared, then plunged. She caught the babe by its tiny skirt and half flung, half pushed it behind her before she and the motor-cyclist came down together in a tangle of limbs and a resounding crash of metal. Then the stutter of the dying engine was drowned in the noisy clamour of shock, blame and sympathy which swelled in direct proportion to the gathering size of the crowd. Hands reached to help Sara to stand. She was supported to the pavement, leaving the motor-cyclist to a wordy wrangle which looked as if it might come to blows. She was dusted down, clucked over and shown by pointing fingers that the errant baby was back in its mother's arms, while Katin nursed the other. Over the heads of the crowd she waved a signal to Katin that she wasn't hurt but that she wouldn't stay any longer. She had paid off her taxi, but another was found

for her and she was bowed away with friendly ceremony.

In the taxi she took stock. Her palms were grazed,
one shoulder ached, and for the first time she was
aware that the long gash from ankle to shin was
the result of that leg's having been pinned under
the weight of the machine. She thanked fortune that
she had had anti-tetanus serum before she left England, but could feel pain and discomfort increasing
by the minute, and knew that, little as her errand
had accomplished, she must abandon it for today.

At home a shocked Malee ran a bath for her and
Buppa supervised the dressing of her leg. Buppa
announced, 'Tuan telephoned while Mem was out;
asked that Mem should call him when she came
back. Mem knows where, he says.'

Sara said, 'Thank you. Yes, I do.' But she had
expected to have time to decide whether to ring
Rede or not, and now she didn't know how much, if
anything, to tell him.

She was still hesitating when the bell rang and
she had to lift the receiver.

'Sara?' Rede's voice.

'Yes. I was out when you rang before, but I did
mean to call you because—well, I think I have a
clue, or perhaps not a clue, more of an idea really,
about where to get news of Mai. That's where I've
been while I was out—following it up.'

'Following Mai up? Where?'

'Not Mai herself—the idea I'd had. Looking for a
man who might know something about her, or even

where she is. That took me to Chinatown——'

'You hared off into *Chinatown* on this crazy hunch you'd had? Why didn't you ring me straight away?' There was biting censure in Rede's tone. 'You had Lim along with you, of course?'

'No. I thought you didn't want the staff to know anything about Mai, so I took a taxi.'

'And——?'

'I'm afraid I didn't learn much. I—had a bit of an accident, you see.'

'What kind of an accident?'

'I was knocked down by a speeding motor-cyclist.'

'You were going on foot in Chinatown? What had become of your taxi?'

'I had paid it off while I called at an address I'd been given. But really, though I had to come home, I'm not much hurt—only some cuts and bruises. Anyway, about Mai——'

'Save it,' Rede cut in. 'You can hang up now. I'm coming back.'

'Tonight? *Can* you?'

'If there's a night plane I should make it by the small hours. And Sara—call Doctor Houland to yourself.'

'Oh, Rede, I'm all right. There's no necessity!'

'*Call* him.' Rede hung up.

He did not arrive in the early morning. He had had to fly via Kuala Lumpur, where the flight had been grounded by fog for over two hours. Sara had just finished dressing when he came into her room. After greeting her, he pointed to her bandaged leg. 'Ought you to be on that? Has Houland seen it?' he asked.

'Yes. He has stitched it and says it will go on all right.'

'And the rest?'

She touched her shoulder. 'Bruising there, that's all.'

'And shock?'

'Some, I expect. But he made me take a sleeping pill, and I'm fine this morning.'

'And these are the facts you didn't give me over the phone?' As Rede spoke, he pointed to a head-lined item on the front page of the copy of the *Straits Times* which he had had under his arm. 'The early edition which I picked up at the airport,' he explained. 'Have they got the details right?'

Sara read the short paragraph which enlarged upon the headline—'Heroic Street Rescue of Child By Wife Of Well Known Citizen', and smiled wryly. 'Most of them,' she said. 'But there was nothing "heroic" about it. This baby ran out into the road; I grabbed her, and that was all there was to it.'

'Except that you may have saved its life and pro-bably risked your own, if I've ever seen a China-town street in the evening. How did they know who you were? Were you badgered by reporters?'

'No. I left as soon as I could get a taxi. But Katin knew who I was. She must have told them I was Mrs Rede Forrest, I suppose.'

Rede's brows went up. 'Katin? The Malaysian

girl who informed on George Merlin?'

Sara nodded. 'And now I believe she could be a lead to Mai.'

'How's that? Did they know each other?'

'No, but——' Sara turned about on her dressing-stool. 'Sit down, Rede, please, and listen——'

He put a question or two into her story as she told it, and when she finished lamely, 'Well, that—finding Katin, I mean—was as far as I got,' he queried dryly, 'And it didn't occur to you that you could have got this Charn Narong's address from your personnel lady, just as easily as you got Katin's?'

Sara's mouth dropped open. 'Oh——!' she said blankly. 'I never thought of that. And now I remember, Katin did begin to ask me why I hadn't, I think. But just then the baby dashed, and——'

'Katin's wits a step ahead of yours, evidently. But if you had been a bit more smartly off the mark, you might have saved yourself from charging into the heart of Chinatown at a peak hour, and getting your name in the papers,' said Rede, his tone still dry.

Sara looked across at him anxiously. 'Rede, I'm sorry about that—about the *Times* getting hold of it. Do you mind very much?'

He came to stand over her, looking down at her. 'Mind?' he echoed. 'Let's say, about as much as any man would mind his wife's showing the world the brand of courage she has.'

'Oh, Rede!' Embarrassed by the oblique compliment, she looked away. 'Anyhow, there was nothing brave about it. It was just a reflex action thing that anyone could have had.'

He agreed, 'The reflex bit, I grant you. The action, no. In nine onlookers out of ten, there'd be either none or too late.'

'Which doesn't prove I was brave at all—only that I was the out-of-step tenth who jumped to it in time.' She glanced at him with a hint of mischief. '*And* is in blank contradiction of your claim that, as to quick-wittedness, Katin has a good deal of edge on me!' she concluded lightly.

The corner of his mouth lifted in wry amusement. 'In other words, I can't have it both ways—either you are as dumb as they come, or you are the original bionic woman? All right. But may I remind you that I didn't suggest the reflex-action theory. *I* only ventured to praise your courage.'

Touched, 'Yes, and thank you. I'm grateful,' she said, thinking as she spoke that she would have thanked a stranger's commendation in much the same words. She and Rede were still worlds apart in everything in which they should have been close.

He was saying practically now, 'And so this is where we take to the only trail to Mai that we've got—this fellow with whom you think you saw her once, and for whom we have a name, if not yet an address.'

'I *know* I saw them together,' Sara claimed. 'Are you going back to Mrs Sunderabad to ask her about him?'

'And you're coming too. You're my credentials for asking questions which the lady might think it her business duty to refuse to answer.' Taking both Sara's hands in his, as if she needed help to stand, he asked, 'Can you walk to the car on that leg?'

'Of course—anywhere.' But she had to accept the support of his arm tucked firmly into hers, and also the surprising intimacy of his fingers feeling for hers and clasping them too.

Only twice in the drive into the city did she question their errand. 'Are you thinking that Mrs Sunderabad might refuse to give you Mr Narong's address?' she asked.

Rede nodded. 'It's just possible. Yesterday you were enquiring about a girl whom you knew. To-day I'm asking about a man I can't claim to know, which is where you will have to satisfy her that the two enquiries are connected.'

'I see.' Later, and just before they reached the store, Sara put her infinitely more difficult query.

'Rede,' she began, 'supposing—that is, if we do find Mai, will you try to be kind? Try not to blame her too much for running away?'

His mouth set in a hard line. 'That's going to depend on how good a reason she had,' he said grimly.

'But she must have had a reason which seemed good to her!' Sara pleaded. To which he retorted,

'Good enough to justify her cheap getaway? It had better be.'

Sara sighed. He had said there had been nothing

of love between himself and Mai. But Mai's letter had implied she had run away from him in person, and could he be so bitter if it weren't so? Sara wondered.

Mrs Sunderabad was so agreeable about supplying the address they wanted that they left the store within a quarter of an hour later, after she had also found time to give Charn Narong a warm testimonial. An excellent employee, conscientious, reliable and with a charming manner towards customers, was her verdict. They drove out to Changi village and Rede stopped the car outside one of the modern purpose-built apartment blocks which faced out over formal garden plots and neat lawns.

The Narong address was on the ground floor. As they waited for their knock to be answered, Sara whispered, 'Supposing he denies any knowledge of Mai?' and Rede replied, 'Then we'll be back to Square One. Just as we shall be if your hunch was wrong and we're chasing a fellow you've never seen in your life.'

But when the door was opened to them, it was by the urbane young waiter of Sara's memory, and hand-in-hand with him was Mai.

CHAPTER NINE

WITH a little gasp, Mai wrenched her hand free and set it palm to palm with the other in greeting. Her head bowed, she murmured, humbly, 'Mr Rede. Mrs Sara,' as if she had never addressed them less formally than that. Then her hand took refuge again in the young man's as she lifted her liquid dark eyes to him. 'Tell them, please Charn. They do not know,' she appealed.

The young man acknowledged Rede and Sara with a slight bow. 'Mr Forrest—Mrs Forrest. I know of you from Kluai Mai. My name is Charn Narong. We are betrothed. This is my father's house. Please to come in.'

He showed them into a bright room where a white-haired woman was sewing. 'My mother,' he introduced her. 'My father works at batik factory and is not here until evening. Kluai Mai will live with us until we are married.' He paused and looked down at Mai's bent head. 'I must tell them now, little one, why you left them and came to us, and that for the wrong you did them, I alone am at fault.'

At that Mai seemed to come to life. 'No!' she protested. 'I must tell them, and they must blame me.' She turned to Sara. 'Please, you will listen and try to understand?'

Sara glanced at Rede's stony expression and thought it best to speak for him. She said to Mai, 'We'd have liked you to tell us the truth before you left us. But yes, we'll listen now.'

Mai betrothed! Her future settled by this self-possessed young man. But did she love him? And what, Sara wondered, were she and Rede to be forced to hear about Mai's desperate bid for escape from the prison of her love for Rede?

Mai sought Charn's hand again and gripped it as she began dispiritedly,

'We are children together in Kota Tingii, Charn and I. We play and learn together and know always that we like to be with each other more than with anyone else. Then, when I am fourteen and he is older, and we have finished with school, his father comes to Singapore for work, and I learn to dance with a teacher. We do not meet very often, but when we do, though we talk always of marriage one day, we are happy to wait for a while.

'For Charn, you see, must first do his sacred service as monk, when he joins the monastery and I may not see him during all his time there and his mendicant journeys. That time began a month before you'— she glanced quickly at Rede and away— 'before you came to Kota Tingii and promised me a place in the Dance School if I passed its tests.'

Rede spoke for the first time. 'You told me nothing about this attachment. Don't you think you should have done?'

She nodded slowly, then contradicted that. 'Not,' she said, 'when I knew how much it meant to you that I should dance. Dance perfectly, give all my time and thinking to the dance, live for dancing—which I could not do.'

Rede accused, 'You allowed me to believe you could.'

'Because I knew how much it meant to you that I should make a great career.'

'A career I've wanted for you, because I know it's well within your powers.'

'And wanting it for me, you would have been ashamed and hurt and disappointed if I had not made it—though I did not want to.'

'If you didn't, you put on a pretty good show of complete dedication to it,' Rede returned acidly.

'To please you, Mr Rede. Only to please you. I love to dance and always shall, but——'

'And you thought I couldn't take the truth? Tell me, do you suppose I've never been disappointed or let down by anyone before?'

For the first time Mai looked him squarely in the face. 'I think it not very likely, Mr Rede,' she said quietly. 'Except by me, I think your trust will always have been honoured. You *expect* it to be, and so it is.'

He shrugged. 'Hm, you'd be surprised. However, you're saying that, though you were afraid to tell me so, your heart never was in your dancing career?'

Shy again, 'Only,' she said, 'the bit of my heart that didn't belong to Charn. And though I was afraid to tell you, I did try to get you to allow me to escape from it——'

'By claiming you weren't equal to it, which was patently nonsense. For pity's sake, child,' Rede suddenly exploded, 'What kind of monster do you take me for, that you dared not tell me the truth, and so took the coward's way out by running away instead?'

'Please, Rede——' That was protest from Sara at sight of Mai's trembling mouth and glistening eyes. But he shook off the hand which Sara had laid on his arm and pulled Mai towards him. Charn reluctantly let her go.

'Why couldn't you stand up to me and tell me that dancing was all very well, but that you were in love and wanted to marry and live happily ever after with your man?' Rede demanded of the girl.

She hung her head. 'I thought you would not understand.'

'About love?' Rede paused. 'Why shouldn't I? I'm married, aren't I?'

Mai looked up and across from him to Sara and back again. Then comprehension seemed to dawn like a lovely light and her slow smile was for them both. 'You mean that because you love each other, however disappointed you were about me, you would have understood and have forgiven me?' she whispered.

'You could put it like that,' said Rede.

They had stayed in the bright little apartment until

the early afternoon. Before Mai had flung herself, first into Rede's arms and then into Sara's with an ecstatic, 'Oh, *Rede*! Oh, Sara *dear*!' the white-haired mother had quietly departed to make coffee, as if confident, even if no one else was, that it would be welcomed by the company before long. After that Sara and Rede were pressed to stay for the midday meal. Mai cooked a dish of *laksa,* and for dessert there were fresh mangoes and diced pineapple in syrup, wrapped in parcels of hot, mouth-melting pastry.

Mai had confided to Sara, 'We shall be married at the new moon—it is a good-fortune time for marriage. We are able to rent a small apartment, and Charn is decorating it with wall-paintings now. He is very clever with his brush.'

'And will you dance at all after you're married?' Sara asked.

'Charn says I may take a few engagements, and I shall. Until'—Mai flushed prettily—'until the babies come, and then I shall be happy to be mother. And as good wife to Charn as you are to Rede. And now he has forgiven me, you will both come to my marriage ceremony?'

Sara had promised that they would, and now, alone with Rede on their return journey to the city, there was nothing between her and her inevitable admission to him of how her doubts had wronged him and Mai; an owning-up to a guilt for which 'I'm sorry' or even 'Forgive me,' would be utterly, emptily inadequate.

He knew of her suspicions and had scorned them with acid force. And yet, right up to Mai's telling of her story, she hadn't had faith enough to believe him. He had called her self-wronged, and so she was. The seeds of Isabel Iden's poison had found fertile ground with her, and how, *how* was she to atone to Rede for that?

The traffic was heavy and he drove in silence until they reached the quiet residential roads of their district. Then he gave her an opening.

'Well, the child certainly fooled me,' he said. 'Talent, dedication, ambition—I thought she had the lot. And what do I find? That I've been playing Svengali, not to a budding world-famous classical *danseuse*, but to a cosy homebody with her sights set no higher than a two-by-four apartment in Changi village, bless her silly heart!' He sounded less angry than wryly self-critical, and Sara was relieved.

She said, 'It was good of you to leave her to the illusion that ours was a—a normal marriage. She would have been utterly shattered if you'd told her the truth.'

'And what is the truth? You wanted your revenge upon Iden; I wanted marriage to you for my own reasons. But did you really expect I'd allow Mai to guess we'd struck the cynical bargain we did?'

'You could have done, and that's why I'm grateful that you didn't.'

'You underrate my discretion.'

'No, your thought for Mai. And perhaps to save *my* face.'

He shrugged. 'As you please. Anyway, how true is it now? Signed and sealed as the agreement was at the time, I'd thought we might tear up both our copies after I'd first claimed you as my wife. But though you co-operated and seemed to enjoy me, it was only with your body. Your heart wasn't among those present.'

'I—— You——!' She blushed furiously.

'Don't deny that your flesh did enjoy it!'

'I found you very—experienced,' she managed.

'But I melted none of the rest of the ice between us?'

'It's always been ice of your making. On occasion you've treated me like a wife; on others, as if I were a stranger.'

'One isn't jealous of a stranger. And I've had enough reason for jealousy.'

'Of Cliff? But you weren't jealous of him for love of me. Only because you thought he was encroaching on your—property.'

They had reached the house and Rede halted the car, but made no move to get out of it. 'On the contrary,' he said, 'I was jealous of Iden for some time before I put in a tender for the property.'

'*Before* you——? Oh no, that's impossible!' she rejected.

'True all the same. From my first sight of the girl who was crying for him at his wedding, I was ready to hate the man who'd driven her to it. Jealousy at first sight, you could call it—over a girl I didn't even know.'

'And when you did know her, you despised her for wanting to pay out the man!'

'I admit her determination for revenge surprised me.'

'And revolted you? But you still proposed marriage to me—why?'

'Because by then I wanted you so much—you *and* your "hell hath no fury" bit against Iden— that I used it to make you the only brand of proposal you'd have entertained from me. Still half in love with him——'

'I *wasn't*!'

'Anyway, not within light years of any feeling for me, cocooned as you were in your bitterness. The only way I could reach you or lay claim to you was to present myself as an ally in your revenge.'

'Which died on me very soon afterwards, if it hadn't already.'

'As I guessed, from your lukewarm effort at "showing" him. So—they've turned each other on again. I told myself, and should be thinking it still if I hadn't more or less blackmailed him before I sent him to Hong Kong.'

'Blackmailed him? *Rede!*'

'In a manner of speaking. I told him I'd take him back into Temasik and give him the Hong Kong job, only at the price of the truth about his relationship with you. He couldn't wait to tell it.'

'And it was——?'

'That Isabel has snared him like a rabbit. He's utterly infatuated, terrified of losing her, worships the ground, etc., etc. And when I put the awkward question as to why I had caught him with you in his arms, he hardly remembered having done it. Had he really? Must have been mad. And then we were back at Isabel's perfections again, and I said "Right, it's a deal. Good luck to you, man." But where did all that get me with you? Nowhere where I hadn't been all along—at the arms' length of your beauty and your dignity and your duty to my social affairs and to Mai, and at the eternal nag of knowing that when I've managed to arouse you against your will, you've seen my worship of your body only as evidence that I'm "experienced" in lovemaking. In any other way that matters in a marriage you've never let me get near you.'

What was he telling her? Sara distrusted her hearing. 'Wanted'. 'Worship'. Spoken of her, what meaning dared she let such words have? She said, 'You've never let me guess you wanted any more of me than the uses for which you married me, and I've tried not to fail you in those.'

'Though without reading any of my need of you into certain of them?'

'You gave no sign of needing me. The first time you—took me, you called me a green girl for supposing you couldn't claim it as your right. And later, when you didn't ask even that of me, I thought it was because you were in love with Mai. That you were showing me you no longer wanted me even as a fillgap in your life.'

'And if you thought that of Mai and me, why did you never accuse me of it until a couple of nights ago?'

Elbows on her hunched knees, Sara sat forward, her hands cupping her face. That way she hadn't to look at him as she confessed, 'Because I was afraid of hearing you tell me that it was so.'

'You mean your pride was afraid? Your status as my wife was afraid?'

'Not my pride,' she whispered. 'That didn't come into it.'

'What then?'

Silence.

'*What then?*' He wrenched her round to face him. '*What* was afraid?'

'My sick jealousy of Mai. My—aching need of you.'

He held her rigidly. With a kind of incredulous wonder he said, 'You were jealous of Mai, but you could still be kind to her for my sake? Because you cared enough for me; wanted me, as I've wanted you?'

'As I've wanted you, loved you ever since——'

'At first sight, as I fell for you?'

She shook her head. 'Not then. But as soon as I realised that if I hadn't married you, I'd have been lost for ever in a kind of desert of regret. You'd despised me for accepting you, but that was the price I had to pay for being near you ... loving you, even if you didn't love me——'

'Didn't love you! Oh, Sara——!' He released her, took both her hands in his and bent over them. She put her lips to his hair, leaned against him, and for long minutes neither of them spoke nor stirred.

Then Rede sat up, facing forward with a hand on the door-handle, and said to her utter dismay, 'I'm going back to Thailand tonight.'

Hurt, bewildered by this cruel anti-climax, 'Oh, Rede! Tonight? Must you?' she pleaded.

He was out of the car by now, coming round to her side. With an arm around her after he had helped her out, he ignored her question to add, 'And you're coming with me.'

'*I* am?'

'Who else?' He fell into step with her as they walked towards the house. 'D'you remember I refused once to take you with me on a stag affair in Rangoon?'

'Yes.'

'Well, this time you're coming along. But this time—no stags in the plural. Just one, with his mate, on the honeymoon they should have had months ago——' He stopped and turned her to him. 'Do you realise we haven't yet kissed as lovers— as *two* people in love and hungry for each other?'

He kissed her then, but only lightly, in teasing promise of the rapture to come.

In the darkness the sea lapped gently at the crescent of sand which was the tiny bay of Tikaya, east of Bangkok. Rede had hired a car at the airport and they were out at the quiet resort within an hour of their flight's landing. The beach itself was their hotel's forecourt and they could step out on to it from the balcony to their ground-floor room.

They had arrived so late that they had been the only diners in the flower-bedecked restaurant, and afterwards they had walked on the sands and had lingered at the water's edge, daring the little wavelets to reach their toes.

They had talked, asked wondering questions, groped through clouds of doubt in search of reassurance.

Once Sara had mused, 'You said you would have thought more of me if I'd refused to marry you. But if I had, I should have lost you.'

'For good, you think?' Rede shook his head. 'I might have applauded your admirable scruples, but you wouldn't have been rid of me so easily. I'd have been back.'

'But *what* made you fall for me?'

'Do you expect me to analyse it? As soon as I saw you, you were there for me—*all* there. Fresh and virginal, but potentially all woman. Hurt and angry woman whom I longed to comfort, if she would let me, which I knew she wouldn't, so I had to approach her by another way.'

'A cynical way!'

'And cynically accepted.'

'No. I snatched at what I saw as my only chance of holding you, though without admitting why I had to.'

'And when did you first know why?'

She had hesitated. 'I think—at the Lotus Room, when you dared me to repeat that I wished you'd never married me, and I couldn't. That night I thought you'd been cruelly designing and unfeeling, but I knew jealousy of you for the first of many times. What had Isabel been to you, I wondered, that you'd had to punish both of us by flaunting us at each other as you did?'

'I thought I was helping you to flaunt your conquest of me at Iden, and I didn't mind if the message got over to Isabel too.'

'Or that I got the wrong message, which Isabel did her best to fill out by taunting me with how close she and you had been?'

'It didn't occur to you to ask her why she hadn't managed to pin me down to marriage while she claimed to have had the chance?' Rede's hand, loosely on Sara's wrist, drew her closer. 'You have been a push-over for jealousy without doing anything about it, haven't you?' he chided gently.

'What could I do, until you told me she'd never meant anything to you?'

'Did it say nothing to you that I'd done my best, for all to see, to marry her to Iden?'

'You could have tired of her, I thought. And before you convinced me there'd been nothing between you Isabel had poisoned my mind about Mai.'

'Ah——What about Mai?'

'Isabel hinted that there was nothing to choose between your relations with Mai and George Merlin's with Katin Char, except that he called Katin his cook, while you, needing to be more discreet, called Mai your protegée.'

There was a sound as if Rede were grinding his teeth. 'Isabel fed you all this and you believed her?' he demanded.

'I tried not to, but in the face of everything——'

'In the face of nothing!' he exploded. 'I believed in the child and I had ambition for her—too much belief and too much ambition in the professional field, as events have proved, and if I'd guessed sooner that your idea that Mai was my mistress was keeping the distance between us, I shouldn't have left you to that misconception for long.'

'And how would you have convinced me otherwise?' As soon as the words were out, she realised how arch they must have sounded when he held her off from him to ask,

'Do you really want to learn how—or are you just playing the coquette?'

'I'd—like to know.'

'Right!' Turning her about, he took her hand to lead her up the beach and to the french window of their room. 'Is this the first night bit where I carry the bride across the threshold?' he asked.

Trembling with excitment, 'It's not our first night together,' she pointed out.

'And this isn't the first time I've carried you to bed,' he retorted. Lifting her effortlessly, he pushed the door-pane with his knee, carried her across the room and sat beside her on the coverlet where he laid her. 'That time,' he reminded her, 'you were in a vixenish temper. What kind of a mood are you in now?'

She said nothing in reply; just looked at him and held her arms wide to him in welcome.

'Ah, love——' His hands moved gently but expertly in search of the soft flesh of her shoulders, bare but for the straps of her square-cut sundress. Her own fingers found and explored the taut muscles of his back beneath his shirt, and male and female bodies shaped to each other, curve to curve and limb to limb.

At first their eagerness was tempered by shyness on both sides. But gradually, at the instance of Rede's tenderness and the gentle, questing touch of his lips and hands, Sara felt desire glow in her blood and turn to flame, and then her response to him was equally a demand, as vivid and alive and urgent as his.

Passion surged and erupted, thrusting them up, up to a peak of ecstasy at the same shared moment before it spent itself and ebbed like a dying cadence of music.

His lips against Sara's closed eyelids, Rede murmured brokenly, 'Loveliness—all loveliness!' and presently they slept.

Sara woke to see and hear Rede crossing the floor to the windows.

'Rede——?'

He turned and beckoned to her. 'Come and look. It's nearly dawn.'

It was. The surface of the sea was still dark, but there was a grey and faintly pink spread of cloud above the horizon and a promise of light between the cloud and the sea.

'Will you swim with me?' Rede asked.

Sara dimpled. 'I didn't bring——' she began.

He grinned. 'Neither did I. I packed in too much of a hurry last night.'

'Then how can we? People will see us.'

'Only a seagull or two, as early as this. Come——'

Hand in hand they ran down the beach, flung aside silk robe and towelling jacket, then waded in guilty haste through the shallows and when they were out of their depth, plunged. They came up laughing, to throw fountains of spray at each other before they plunged again.

Water-babies. Boy and girl. Man and woman. Mates ...

And there's still *more* love in

Harlequin Presents...

Yes!

Six more spellbinding
romantic stories every month
by your favorite authors.
Elegant and sophisticated tales of
love and love's conflicts.

Let your imagination be swept away to
exotic places in search of adventure,
intrigue and romance. Get to
know the warm, true-to-life
characters. Share the special
kind of miracle that
love can be.

Don't miss out. Buy now and discover
the world of HARLEQUIN PRESENTS...

What readers say about Harlequin Romances

"I feel as if I am in a different world every time I read a Harlequin."
  A.T.,* Detroit, Michigan

"Harlequins have been my passport to the world. I have been many places without ever leaving my doorstep."
  P.Z., Belvedere, Illinois

"I like Harlequin books because they tell so much about other countries."
  N.G., Rouyn, Quebec

"Your books offer a world of knowledge about places and people."
  L.J., New Orleans, Louisiana

"Your books turn my...life into something quite exciting."
  B.M., Baldwin Park, California

"Harlequins take away the world's troubles
and for a while you can live in a world of
your own where love reigns supreme."
L.S.. Beltsville. Maryland

"Thank you for bringing romance back
to me."
J.W.. Tehachapi, California

"I find Harlequins are the only stories on
the market that give me a satisfying
romance with sufficient depth without
being maudlin."
C.S.. Bangor. Maine

"Harlequins are magic carpets...away from
pain and depression...away to other people
and other countries one might never know
otherwise."
H.R.. Akron. Ohio

*Names available on request